A Goddamn Infinite Emergency

Love Stories

John Mandel

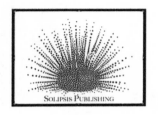

SOLIPSIS PUBLISHING

Published by Solipsis Publishing
1947 Broadway E.
Seattle, WA 98102

Cover Art: John Mandel
Cover Design: Rafe Mandel

A Goddamn Infinite Emergency/ John Mandel

Print Edition ISBN 978-0-9978436-0-6

To R, M, L, J

CONTENTS

One

❧

THE GENIUS OF TOUCHING ME

1

A man comes to see my wife once a week. I think he is an advisor. She has involvements with institutes, and I'm certain that he was sent by one of them, because he seems so much like a man from an institute—suited, immaculate, cool as a mandarin.

I don't like it at all. I think he might be advising her that the only thing that stands in the way of achieving her goals—and that prevents her from embracing the idea he's peddling to help her achieve them—is *me*; that without me and my infinite gloom, my goofy predicaments, she might realize her potential. Or another institute might suggest she become a devotee of something that will consume her absolutely, and I'll be abandoned. A third institute might suggest she become a bride of Jesus instead of *my* bride, goddamnit, for all I understand about what's happening. I don't know what he's telling her, and I'm afraid to ask; although I'm bookish and I try to think deeply about things, it will be something I won't be able to understand no matter how many times it's explained to me. And I think she'll hear the fear in my voice, assume I'm suggesting that something is being done to me, and become angry.

I don't like it, and I don't like the man.

My wife and I have a fundamental disagreement about the nature of things. I tell her I like common sense. I like truth like a rock. Give me the existential life, I tell her. Life is hard enough, I say, trying to find a reasonable and safe path through the thousand tons of data streaming past us as we make our way through a room, through a day. I tell her that I think the world is so simple, as simple as breathing. Hard, but as simple as pushing a big rock up a hill; just open your eyes, all the way, I tell her, and you'll see it. I always get a little forceful, wanting to shake her into my way of thinking, into the room, into my arms. "*Be here now*, for chrissake," I might say—if I'm feeling brave.

But she is unshakable. She insists that everything is

ephemera. She thinks that nothing is as it appears, that we move through an infinity of holograms (an institute for each one). Alright, holograms, I think, that makes sense; but an infinity of them? What about a last one, one last dreamy figment of a good and reasonable life before the figment evaporates? There it is—you'll know just what to do.

Her way of thinking seems to be just asking for it, a straight line to melancholia. How will she know when it's time to rest? How will she know when it's time to be happy?

And what would I do in the minutes after I accept that there is no substance to being—shoot myself?

But when we discuss our points of view, I hear her fine brain at work, exegesis in an angel's voice, sweet breath from the cherry bud of a mouth. I start to sway to her way of thinking and that gives me vertigo, and that makes me uneasy, and that makes me want to pinch her hard, hear her yelp, watch a red mark appear, and say: So that's it, isn't it? That was real, wasn't it? You're in the world, that's all there is, let's eat.

Of course, I've never pinched her, and I never *would* pinch her, or harm her in any way, or even raise my voice, except in a sudden, explosive soliloquy about my love for her—, because I do love her so much. And, anyway, I'm a goddamn mess;, why would anybody listen to *my* ideas? A first principle: Never read a philosopher who killed himself.

After their first meeting I saw her crumple up and throw away an envelope the man had left. Later when she left the room I tiptoed to it and retrieved it, locked myself in the bathroom, smoothed it out on the counter, and studied it. There is a little picture of a skyscraper in the upper left-hand corner, and next to it, the man's name, Philippe something, in raised letters. I'm not reassured about an institute that would have a skyscraper for its symbol. I don't think I'm being ridiculous; the choice of a skyscraper absolutely signifies some kind of conceit, some evidence that they assume they're invincible and immortal. What chance would I have against something like *that*? After all, what would *my* symbol be? A pissy flower? A man languishing in bed?

Every week, when I know the man is about to arrive, I push my big stuffed chair across the room up to the window, make myself comfortable, and study him through the little opening in the curtain as he walks up the path toward the front door. I'm always startled by how much he himself seems like a skyscraper: very tall and rigid, aloof, with a little cowlick that could be the spire. The back of his neck is shaved high and pale and is lavender like a priest's, and his face is conventionally handsome, but with an odd cast, as though it had been reconstructed after an accident. But somehow it works, giving him character, and this is bad news, because when I've nervously asked my wife the obligatory questions about what kind of man she is attracted to in general, hoping to hear something that *I* might offer, character is always the first and most important attribute, and she makes it clear that very little else will contravene this quality. When I first saw the man, seeing the worst, I ran to the bathroom mirror and locked myself in to look for character in my own face. I wasn't reassured; I looked like a man at a window watching somebody run up the path shouting bad news.

The advisor's personality is unreadable. His real nature is sunk into the Institute, into the job. He doesn't seem predatory, but if I get close enough to the window while he waits on the porch, his face will be no farther than a few inches away from mine; if I could get a good look into his pupils, I know I'd see it.

When he rings the bell, a sound now saturated with apprehension, I leap out of my chair and run away so my wife doesn't see that I've been studying him. Before she answers the door, she finds me (she always knows where to find me) and asks me if I would mind waiting in the tiny courtyard outside the back door of the apartment while she has her meeting with him. Their meeting needs to be private, she explains, that's always the way this kind of thing is done, and if *you* had a visit by a man from an institute, she continues, I would understand immediately about the need for privacy. She isn't asking me to leave the apartment altogether, she says, which she understands wouldn't be very fair, because it's my home, too, and I have every right to be wherever I want to be in it, but if I could only see my way to cooperate, just about this one thing? She always adds that if it gets chilly, or starts to rain, of course, don't hesitate, come right in. I always regard that as kindly, but I know I would freeze to death or drown before I came in on my own.

When she speaks, I don't really listen to the words anymore, only for the sentiment revealed in her tone of voice, her inflection, and that's all I want to know. She makes her small voice go up at the end of the sentence, like a question, to make it seem as if it's *my* decision, which it isn't, it can never be, but I'm grateful and moved by the gesture. I'm dizzy with gratitude, and in any case I'm always spellbound by her eyes, the genius and clarity in them, and her girly face, and her boyish slip of a body.

While she talks to me she walks me out through the back door with her hand on the small of my back. I'm much bigger than she is, and her hand is very small and very delicate (I get tears in my eyes, seeing it), but she drives me like a beast of burden. The pressure of her hand is just right to get the job done without hurting my feelings. She is The Genius of Touching Me.

She says she'll come and get me as soon as the man is gone. As we talk, I think of him waiting at the front door, absolutely still, waiting for her, lizard-like, perhaps not even blinking. I think he waits patiently knowing she's busy getting me out the back door. Nevertheless she always speaks to me so sincerely and so sweetly that I do what she asks without protesting. Even though she repeats the same thing every week, in exactly the same way, with all the same inflections, she always sounds completely earnest to me. I'm happy to do it. "*I'm happy to do it!*" I nearly shout, enthusiastically, meaning it.

Then the door closes on me, making two worlds, mine

without her in it, hers without me in it.

Does she love me? Once, she pushed her pretty face into the hollow of my neck and whispered I love you, I love you, I love you. I thought the first was obligatory, to be kind, the second compensatory for a moment of doubt, and the third a simple sentiment, a simple enthusiasm. I heard it, I know it, she loves me.

2

The first time the man came to see my wife, I stood in the courtyard and looked through the wrong end of the peephole in the back door to the tiny image of them sitting in the living room. They sat on opposite ends of the couch; I could see all of her from my point of view, but I could only see his crossed leg, and occasionally, when he gestured to make a point, I could see a hand. My wife sat still and listened, with her hands modestly folded in her lap. I could hear the tone of his voice, if not the content; everything seemed to be within the limits of propriety.

From my place behind the curtain, I had seen him pat his hair in his rearview mirror before he left the car and walked up the path to the front door. He regarded himself in the little mirror, trying on different expressions, and seemed to choose one. As an expert student of how best to adore my wife, I knew, hopelessly, that he'd chosen the right one.

Perhaps when the man sent her the literature with the image

of the skyscraper, he hoped it would make her subconsciously think of an erect penis; he waits a week or two, while the thought swells in her into a little underground river of desire, and then he shows up, skyscraper-like, to drink from her.

"If God loves me . . . " the man thinks, as he walks up the path.

But maybe he isn't so overtly conscious of a strategy, maybe he himself is only subconsciously aware of the phallic quality of the skyscraper, or even of his desire to be intimate with my wife. Instinctually he likes it as a symbol for himself; it seems distinguished, and inspiring, and sturdy, all the ways he would like to be thought of, as an advisor and a man, and he sends it to her to herald his qualities. Then I think of what I witness as a kind of epic morality play; I watch the image in the peephole as if it were a tiny puppet theater: two mortals taken by the Byzantine mysteries of the human embrace.

I was very agitated as I watched them the first time; wouldn't he notice just how lovely she is? Isn't she so lovely that he would soon have to reckon with the fact of it? Wouldn't he, taking that mesmerizing path, inevitably think about her vagina? I don't judge the man, how could he not? It's certainly what *I* have a tendency to do, no matter how hard I try not to. I've stood on the sidewalk discussing current events with the nice Episcopalian lady next door; I act like a good man, trying to appear as if I'm listening closely, I furrow my brow, I stroke my chin, making the attendant sounds of thoughtfulness— while I'm thinking the most debased thoughts, wondering about the vagina of the woman, its qualities, its spectacle. I try to fight the thought, but the holy thing swims up from the monkey brain anyway, like an unearthly blossom.

I gaped at my wife through the little peephole. How could a man not want to kiss this pretty face? What man wouldn't burn up at her spectacle? There's no other way of thinking about it; as night follows day, the man from the Institute will consider briefly or at length my wife's vagina. He'll sit across from her on the sofa, speaking earnestly to her in the measured voice of the Institute; but in time she'll crash into his brain, he'll feel dizzy and his voice will go up octaves. Dazed, he wanders home to a sleepless night. The world is new. Then he must act, he must make it manifest, it can't be helped; it's the law of men.

I watched them through the peephole. Suddenly they simultaneously adjusted their bodies for comfort; they appeared slightly to move toward one another, and time slowed—I waited an eternity to see if the motion would continue forward into an embrace. It didn't; as yet the man's manner is seamlessly professional. I haven't seen him cross a line. But what if, above the clothed leg, where I can't see him, his shirt is pulled up and his pants are down and he's wiggling his tongue and penis at her? I'm left to watch *her* for signs of impropriety: erect nipples, or squirming, or blushing, or dilated pupils, or beads of sweat.

I try to think about how *I* might send secret messages of love across the colossal gap of an inappropriate situation, how

I might take the great preemptive leap; but all I can ever think of doing is collapsing to the ground to confess, to shriek my infinite love, tears and spit flying.

I understand that my wife's happiness would, by extension, serve the cause of my own, but I still imagine that one day I won't hear any sound from inside the house for a long time, and when I burst through the door I'll find them gone, with all the food.

3

So I sit.

I sit on the little armless straight-backed chair in the tiny courtyard, with my hands on my knees, and wait for a thousand years. I only think about love as I sit; hot love, god-love, wholesome love, absolute love. I close my eyes and concentrate; I send hot darts of love from the center of my forehead, through the back door, through the rooms, through the man, between her eyes to her brain. *The love-blast radiates her brain, saturates her consciousness, and blooms in her face; her lips swell and part, her eyes cross slightly and begin to roll up. The man sees it, he sees the holy love to which he can only be a pilgrim; he rises from my couch quietly, leaving my pretty wife, walks on tiptoe across my floor, opens my door, and steps out of my house. MINE.*

As I sit I have a regular fantasy of redemptive love, a love conceived in the blasted landscape saturated by my wife's absence, a work in progress:

. . . I get up from my chair and walk into the house, into the room where they're having their meeting. I walk like a busy man, an important man, the man who gets the job done. They look up startled, and as I sail past them I deliver a single slap in tandem across their faces; a hammer– blow for him, and a fake movie slap for her, because I could never slap her pretty face, or hurt her in any way. I run out the front door, down the steps into the street, through the city to the airport; I fly to a country of men and women like myself, where the timid are regarded as saintly and full of character. In this place love streams to me through an umbilical of like-mindedness; everyone wants to glad-hand me and kiss me. I am their president, their bashful president, elected by my constituents because I was the most timid of all the candidates. When I go up to the podium to make a speech, the people and I are all so shy we turn our faces down and away from one another, blush, and clear our throats and shuffle our feet for a long time, until my aides embrace me, comfort me by whispering expressions of love and support, and I can bring myself to make my speech in a high, trembling voice. I speak to them about kissing, fondling, and words of endearment, about how I hugged the ambassador from an African republic, how good it felt when the premier of China slapped me on the back, how warm his hand was and how sincere his slap seemed, how the delegate from the Vatican and I kissed each other on both cheeks, and how we didn't want to stop. I'm a bomb of love, a rolling sphere of love; the world is remade for me as I move through it, like a percussion wave that precedes me ...

4

Our tiny courtyard is one of many that constitute a warren inside the city block. The walls are high; I've tried to jump up to see the other courtyards but I can't jump high enough. My arms are too weak to pull myself up, and I don't own a ladder. I'm left to imagine who else might inhabit the warren; but I can hear them, and I've begun to make a kind of shadow world while I wait for my wife to come and tell me the man has gone.

I can hear an angry man being abusive to someone; when he shouts I get very agitated and have elaborate fantasies of rescuing a frail wife and skinny, sober children. One day I couldn't stand it anymore; I lost my temper and screamed, "*Shut up!*" There was a moment of stunned silence in the warren. I had surprised myself; I realized I was safe from him and screamed it again. I strutted in full display behind the safety and anonymity the high wall provided me; why couldn't *I* be a heavy motherfucker for a couple of goddamn minutes out of a goddamn lifetime? "*Shut up!*" I screamed a third time, so hard I sounded like a little girl. "*Leave them alone!*" I shouted. The man bellowed like a large animal; I picked up a dirt clod and threw it furiously in the general direction of his voice; it, which must have broken up and rained down everywhere, because the whole warren of little courtyards went berserk with shouts and wails. Let the whole world feel the terrible fire of my righteousness, I thought, pacing wildly and stamping my feet, sending up dust clouds and choking on them. "*Leave them alone!*" I shrieked again. Then, suddenly, predictably, I felt ashamed of myself, realizing I knew nothing about the man. I slowed and stopped. Maybe nobody listens to him; maybe even his babies treat him badly. Maybe he has a tumor. "*I'm sorry!*" I shouted.

There is a woman who cries all the time; I think she shares my back wall, because she sounds so close. She cries to her girlfriends about men; they don't love her the right way, they don't love her at all. Her cries are so poignant, so *femme*, I think, so why don't they love her? How could they not love her? Are they stupid?

Sometimes her cries move me, and I cry with her, but I synchronize my sobs with hers so she can't hear me. I press my body against the wall and cry. From an architectural view, above, the crying woman is no more than a foot away from me on the other side of the wall; she looks out into another direction, another hallucination, one without me in it, I can never be in it; and my wife and the man, rooms away, sit on the couch regarding one another intensely, oblivious to me.

There is a little death in the fathomless moment when you realize you're in the mind of no one.

Finally I exhaust myself. I sit with my eyes closed, empty my mind, and wait for the sound of her footsteps to enter the lowest register of my hearing; they appear, they get steadily louder and louder as she comes near, each step a century, and at last the door is thrown open to frame her perfect perfectness.

5

One day, I leaned against the door, watching my wife and the man through the peephole. I was keeping a vigil, but as time went on and nothing happened, my eyes got heavy and I started to fall asleep standing up; suddenly I came fully awake when I realized a rigid finger was being pointed at my wife, like a little hard phallus, to make a point. She seemed to rear back; she stared at it, eyes wide, transfixed, drew in a sudden breath, and blushed. His lacquered fingernail caught the light, a brilliant, blinding laser into my brain; I hurled myself through the door and stampeded through the hallway at them. They looked up, startled, just as I threw myself at the man. My eyes were shut tight and I slapped at him with my open palms as hard as I could.

With a shout he threw up his arms to protect himself. We snarled and cursed and slapped faces and pulled hair and spat and cried and careened around the room. Suddenly we broke apart; we jumped up and stood and regarded one another for a long moment, breathing hard and blinking. I looked into his frightened face, and felt immediately guilty; again, I thought, what do I know about this man and his circumstances? All the events and the order of events in all the generations of his genus and his species and his race and his lineage and all the weather patterns and tectonic plate movements and belief systems and catastrophes and geopolitical movements and wars and revolutions and happenstance in every history on every landmass and every body of water had brought this man to this nature and this place and this moment. What chance did he have to be otherwise? How can someone be something other than what they've become?

"*Oh, god, I'm so sorry,*" I cried out, and stepped up to straighten the little spire-like cowlick, which had collapsed, crestfallen, during the fight. I fussed with it, trying to prop it up, and as I did his skinny fist, horned with sharp knuckles, drew back in a high, calculated arc, ordained to deliver me from my senses. It seemed to come to me very slowly; I was certain I first felt the hairs on the plane of his fist, a little ticklish, then the membrane of skin, soft and warm, then the little pads of fat, then the cartilage, and finally the bone, bone to bone with stupendous finality, sending seismic tremors through all the nerves and ganglia and fissures and rifts back fifteen million years to the thick, dimwitted brain stem, far from the anarchy outside the layers of cartilage, flesh, and carefully combed hair, where nothing is known about the Institute, or my pretty wife, or who is the righteous man. Struck there, my senses convulsing, I flew out of my body to a planet where I could think things I could never conceive of on earth.

I awoke in the late afternoon, curled on the little oval rug in front of the sofa; my wife sat on the floor next to me, watching, holding a cold washcloth to my forehead. The man seemed to be gone. I looked up, lovesick, into her clear, alabaster face, empty of blame, framed by our attractive home, our comfortable furniture, our beautiful paintings, our good food.

Oh, goddamn perfect joy, I thought, what a wife.

Two

❧

The Bleeding Flaneur

Every day, inside my gate on the little concrete pad, in the shadow of the high wooden fence, I lie prone on my cheap chaise lounge. Lying there, I might look like I'm dead, or like a toppled statue of a hero.

Prone is my way. I don't really understand any other way, and I have no patience for the idea of keeping myself busy until I drop dead of exhaustion. Why people bother to do most of what they do is a mystery to me. Why not lie down if you can?

On my lounge, every day, I read and think about things—I

rage and sleep. I lie right outside the front door of my house
and read the newspaper from end to end. I read everything,
anything that drifts my way, I read and read, trying to figure out
how things work, trying to find a lesson coiled in stories, the
menace behind a thin skin of civility, or a scrap of something
redemptive. Good luck to me.

"Nothing is as it seems," an older man said to me when
I was a little boy. I was in my room; there were guests in the
house, filling it with blue cigarette smoke, and the older man
wandered in. He loomed in the tiny room like a hand in a
dollhouse, moving through it, picking up one object after
another and studying it as if he'd never seen such a thing. I was
a very precocious boy, and I had a little library; he examined
it as he moved, showing special interest in my favorite book,
Why, Mom?: Philosophy for Preteens.

"Nothing is as it seems," he said at last with a kindly grin,
waving the book around as if he was making a speech. I gaped
at him.

"What do you mean?" I asked him.

"Just that," he said, "Nothing is as it seems. You're on your
own in this life, kid."

I started to cry at the implications of his lesson; even
then I imagined a purposeless, awestruck life scratching for
a foothold in a churning universe of figments. It was late
afternoon; I rubbed my fists in my eyes and sniffled in the
darkening room while he stared at me.

I've lived in the wake of what the old man told me ever since. I imagine all the things and events in the world as a boiling, incomprehensible mire. I bring food to my mouth. I draw the blanket over myself. My jaw hangs open like an idiot; that's my undivided response to the fathomless world.

Only occasionally does something make sense. I can't really explain; I know it when I see it. For a moment I've entered the slipstream, I'm in the swim.

And everywhere I go there seems to be an oversized man filling the room.

I exhaust myself on the lounge, and then I sleep like I'm dead. Behind me, inside, are my books, my major and minor appliances, my dog and her pillows and bones, my exercise equipment, my vitamins and potions, my contracts and my knick-knacks, my doo-dads and my documents, my food and clothing, scraps of paper with people's addresses on them.

On the chaise lounge, my eyes almost crossed in concentration, I compose furious letters to the editor; this will do it, I think, just the right ideas in just the right order, articulated perfectly, and word will spread exponentially; the people will pour out of their homes and offices and factories to embrace a new regime of reason and good will. Inevitably I have fantasies about being powerful. In them I'm the man that gets things done, a working-class hero. I make a speech. I'm always very handsome and the people always love me (they're *my* fantasies, and I will have them exactly as I want them, humility notwithstanding). Here is one, a work in progress:

A siren sounds somewhere in the city. It's for me, clearing the streets for my parade, rushing to me. I mount the stupendous red gleaming fire truck and wave to the citizens like a beloved revolutionary, or a prodigal son, looking above the mass of them into their levitated minds. What's the difference, I think, when I cast my sunbeams on the people, my spectacle blooming in their love, if I'm a sublime idiot? Or an incubus? Or an all-star? Or a goat-boy?

Men and boys have started to dress like me. Unconsciously they've begun to move like me. As I'm driven slowly through the city, high on the fire truck, gripping the high-ladder hose like a big phallic totem to keep from falling, I look down at the crowds bounding like happy dogs, an army of selves, a body of connubial happiness of which I am the heart, their eyes fixed on mine as they bound. Then we'll sing together, an anthem or a work-song, I and the plasma pool of selves as far as the eye can see, in resonant baritones and gesturing in perfect synchrony.

I'm a crier. If there is a general idea that men don't cry, this one cries his eyes out. A story of a lost pet or genocide or a kid with a tumor will make me cry on my lounge, sometimes so loud I know the woman on the other side of the fence can hear me; I can hear that she's stopped moving, and I stop crying right away. I jump up and hold my breath and put my ear to the fence. I can tell that she does too; we're no farther than an inch from one another on each side of the fence, paralyzed and listening. As I press my ear to the fence, my imagining of her is romanticized by the soft and fragrant vine that covers it: she's pink, and small and lovely, and she smells sweet, like the blossom. I have a fantasy about a kiss; in it I embrace her, she's small in my arms, I bend her back, look into her eyes for a moment, and feel her body go limp in a swoon as I move in for the kiss.

When I see her in the street, I'm always surprised to see that she's a big woman, sulky and unapproachable. Nevertheless, I always greet her aggressively, trying to engage her, trying to get her to acknowledge me and the important thing that's happening between us, but she won't respond. She walks right by me, paying no attention at all, as if I'm just a little shit, a nothing.

Enlightenment

My lumpy dog pads out ritually, only after I've stopped squirming and have settled in on the lounge to the heart of my inquisitions. She sits in front of the chaise lounge at my feet with her back to me, nose to her crack in the fence. From my point of view, my feet flank her fool's ears. She appears to ruminate in her dog's way; she smells the world to reckon with it, separating friends from enemies. When a good poignant odor is picked up, whether it means murder or love, she stands up suddenly and snorts; her tail goes up rigidly, revealing to me her rectum, surrounded visually by my shoes. It looks like an appropriate coat of arms. Consequently, I've come to know something's up in the outside world when I see her rectum, a reasonable herald of what lies on the other side of the fence, given my acerbic view of men and things. A dog's rectum is the puckered lens through which I regard the sorrowing world.

I study the dog. She sleeps what seems to be a holy sleep, twenty-three hours a day. She wakes up for an hour to eat, receive love, and defecate. I provide good food and an occasional caress and I follow behind and clean up her shit as if she were a holy woman. Then back to sleep, like a godhead. According to my Buddhist studies, the dog exhibits all the features of enlightenment. Why think? Why question the beauty of a perfect plan?

Unlike her, as *Homo sapiens sapiens* I'm doomed not only to think, but to think about thinking, and then think about that, and then about that, a brain wrapped into itself as tight as a dreadlock. It's a plan that leads straight to melancholy. *Nothing is as it seems,* the old man had said.

But I'm full of love. Love always lingering hopefully for a host. I'm for love. Hosannas, jubilations, high fives, benedictions to love. May we all have love.

I try to put it off as long as I can but finally, cowering, holding my breath, I go through the gate, out into the rest of the planet to walk the dog. Every day I'm immediately shouted at in greeting by the man across the street, who seems to be there all the time, as if he's lying in wait only for me. The man wants to befriend me, but I don't want it; it's clear by my body language and my cold greeting that I don't want it, but he won't give up. I can see he's one of those smarmy, neutered men who choose to think the best of people, that human beings are essentially good, and if I let him close to me, I will certainly disabuse him of that.

I use a long stick to pull my newspaper in under the gate in the mornings so I won't have to be seen and shouted at. The man sees the stick; I can see him through the crack in the gate and I watch him watching it.

He is a beefy man, a face flat like a shovel, with tiny eyes, a little snub nose, and a mouth so small only a straw might fit into it. He doesn't seem to have any secondary sex characteristics. I think of pictures I've seen of parent killers. He's naturally sociable; hiding behind my curtain, I watch him accost every neighbor he can as they pass with any proximity, drawing them in like a shill on the street. Some of them move past him as fast as they can, with a curt, uncivil greeting like mine, or cross the street strategically. I study them, too, for signs of like-mindedness. But he seems to have some regulars, always men, with names like *Chuck,* hearty glad-handers who stop and pass the day with him. I watch them through the crack in the gate; I can't hear the content, but I watch them roll and parry and posture and provoke each other to greater heights of meaty manliness, booming basso laughs like animal calls meant to be heard far away, and high-fives, hard, stinging slaps like gunshots that make me wince behind the gate.

One is short and wiry, an outlaw; I think of cockfights. I study him through my crack in the fence. He looks as though he's been torn up and sewn back together badly. Even from my distance, I can see his eyes are predatory. I've known men like him, hurt men in an infinite rage, feral and paranoid. The man is fabulous and exotic to me; I'm enthralled by his little moves, the way he makes slit-eyes when he takes a drag on his cigarette, held between thumb and pointer. He makes me wish I smoked. I squirm thinking I want to be like him, for just one day; I want to feel what it is to tell somebody to go fuck their mother.

I've spoken to acquaintances about the man; I always say I think that he will someday go berserk and "take a lot of people out." I like to hear myself say this; I like the sound of it, as though I move with bad men in a parallel universe.

I spoke to him once, and when I did, I tried to bring a tough note into my voice and helplessly slipped into his mannerisms, his languid posture, thrilled by the opportunity to be an outlaw for a moment. We leaned on the car and talked pussy, we talked about The Man, and how we will fuck . . . .him . . . . . . *up.*

Another man, a tall, fit, and handsome one, might be the one who lives in the house with the broken window; I crane my neck as he leaves to see if that's where he goes, but he always disappears around a bend. The window has been broken for as long as I can remember. I try not to read it symbolically, but inevitably it makes me think about bad lives. I don't like to pass the house; subconsciously, I think the broken window is a sign that violence will suddenly bloom from the doorway and envelop me.

I realize as I pass the house that I imagine a shadow figure; I think about someone like this man, a tall man in good shape, a silent, handsome man who stalks through dark rooms with a man's accoutrements. I imagine that he has a single friend, also handsome, with whom he trades mock punches, to sublimate repressed sexual desire.

Once, as I passed the house, I heard a woman's laughter from inside; I was shocked, having assumed that the man moved in an exclusively male ethos. I tried to imagine the woman, first thinking of someone with a big, round, blank face and a halter top. But I have rigorously trained myself to be very suspicious of first ideas, to believe they are likely to be conventional; so at last I visualized her as a wealthy and urbane woman aroused only by trouble, attracted to men who live on the social periphery. This appealed to my own attraction to women in trouble, and I came to have elaborate love and rescue fantasies about her, ultimately unsatisfying because they always compulsively end with a scene in which, having rescued her, I stalk back and forth in front of her, ranting and crying jealously about her having lived the life she did before her rescue. *"How could you!"* I shout.

The woman's laughter had loomed large; now I pass the house as though I had a trace memory of a difficult dream I can't shake about a man who hurts a fragile, good woman, one with whom I'm in love; this, at least, is my analysis of the heartache I experience whenever I pass.

Another man watches with me; he looks out on the shouting man from his window next door or he wanders out to pluck a weed for camouflage. I saw him speaking to the shouting man over the fence once; he stood without moving, unreadable, as the man waved his arms around enthusiastically.

For a short time a beautiful woman lived with him. He's a dour man with a single thick eyebrow and very wide hips; he might have been attractive once, but not anymore. I was happy for the man; I liked the idea of a plain man getting a break with women, and I liked the idea of a dizzy love story in close proximity.

I thought about them all the time; it never stopped being peculiar that the beautiful woman was with such a plain man, which was a source of tension as I passed the house, feeling that only a reasonable explanation of their extreme difference would make it last.

Late one night as I stood outside the gate for a smoke, the beautiful woman drove up with a small U-Haul attached to the rear of her car; she got out, ran into the house, and came out quickly, dragging a sack of personal belongings; she threw it violently into the trailer, jumped in the car, and drove away, tires squealing, the trailer rocking wildly. The scene stunned me; I stood gaping in the dark for a long time, as if the woman had left *me*, and not the man. Any drama of abandonment was an empathic one for me, and it left me agitated and sleepless that night, sensing a crack in the world.

Now, as I pass the man's house, I think only about

absence. I'm certain that the man has had his last kiss, his last endearment, his last chance for the sacrament of love; he has nothing to offer, he'll never have a woman again.

I don't postulate that the man might enjoy being alone, a condition incomprehensible to me; I think of a dirty, solitary man wandering slowly from room to room every day, hoping he'll come upon something of significance in one of them, and always finding nothing. I conceive of a mind observing only itself, leaving the face slack and absent of all social propriety. The man is my patron saint of Loss, a carrier of my fear of abandonment.

I've come to regard the house as shrine-like, and the man as luminous and beautiful.

The men swagger away. I don't like men very much, the way they swagger, moving through an epic daydream of their own making; after any encounter with them, including men behind counters, I'm just grateful that I hadn't wept openly or passed out in front of them, relieved that I didn't vomit or shit myself, or drop to the ground inert and not moving no matter what until someone comes to get me. It's a goddamn odyssey to go out through the gate to buy a carton of milk, to move through streets filled with posturing men and boys, and if I can find a reason, I go right back inside to the deep funk and asylum of my house, which blooms from me like a thought-balloon.

But finally, if I'm to have a life, I must face the shouting man. I tried to slip soundlessly through the gate but the dog's nails tapped on the concrete, giving me away, and the man looked up.

"Buddy! Hey! Look! It's a beautiful morning!" he bellowed across the street to me. As he shouted, he threw his arms up like Atlas holding the world and pointed his big ham of a face up to the sun.

"*Bee-YOU-tee-ful!*" he shouted in four syllables. "C'mon! Whaddaya think?!"

I'm upset enough already by the spectacle of a big man shouting at me every morning, and have come to think of him as a threshold guardian, the first evidence of all the small catastrophes rushing blindly and witlessly at me every day. But the man has the wide-open face and glinty eyes of a religious zealot; therefore I think he wants to instruct me in some kind of positive life view, full of half-baked logical fallacies and platitudes and non sequiturs, and he can just forget about that. He'd better try to make some goddamn sense if he wants to speak to *me*. I regard myself with open conceit as a man who makes up his own mind, and I have no interest in the ideas of other people regarding my nature or the nature of things.

I'm offended that he calls me "buddy," which I regard as a presumption and an unsolicited intimacy. I'm not someone who has ever been regarded as a buddy. My etymology book says the word has something to do with pirates; if the man opened his eyes, he'd see that I'm neither a buddy nor a pirate. I think as a first principle everyone should be very careful about what they say; they should know what they're saying, and especially what they're shouting. I always try to say just what I mean; I have my thesaurus and my dictionaries, my etymologies, my Buddhist studies, my book of classical logical fallacies, and all my readings, the tools I use to just barely manage a delirious universe.

The man's wife, a foreign woman who reproduces rapidly, oversees what seem to me like hundreds of babies on their front lawn; the swarm grows alarmingly with each period of gestation. The man also has babies under both thick arms; like him, they have thick arms and big round faces with tiny features. They're all indistinguishable to me, all with what seem to be standard, bulging, chapped foreheads and little identical gobbets of snot tucked under their snub noses, and all of them, all day and late into the night in the warm season, screech and run back and forth to no purpose, but always with a certain ruthlessness. Slaps and kicks are ubiquitous. Stuffed bunnies and dollies are used as killing implements. Quarrel is their culture; inches of territory, dirt clods and bottle caps are currency, fought over bitterly. Guttural baby shouts ring out and all of them cry all the time. They vomit and shit spontaneously, without social consciousness. Dirt is eaten and spit flies indiscriminately. The fecund wife, her own face—a divinity like the sun worshipped by the man—beams as she shepherds. Every punched face, every mind-altering shriek, every unscheduled bowel movement causes her smile to deepen beatifically. The world is as it should be; a race of unspanked babies streaming from her boggy womb, filthy in their own effluvia, carrying her traits and ideas and ways, cells splitting exponentially, eternally. The shouting man husbands the herd, and the sun that makes everything beautiful for the man warms and illuminates the world of their own making. God is good.

I think he's a good man; his fruited wife and his thousand babies are happy and healthy, evidence of a man's goodness. But I wonder why he's blind to *my* spectacle; why he doesn't see what any kid could see in my face: that I'm being flayed by devils, I'm eating myself alive, and that I don't have any beautiful days. The man makes me angry; I believe that if he opens his eyes, if he's so goddamn benevolent, he'll take one look at me and rush across the street to embrace me. He'll cradle me on my front lawn, and as he pets my head he'll tell me everything will be alright, that he will see to it. He'll try with all his might to find the right words to explain how I might grasp the concept of a beautiful day.

I'll never speak to the man; but I'd like to explain to him that the world is an incomprehensible, finite catastrophe, that even the pretty smiles on the faces of his hundred thousand babies are suspicious; that man is a graceless, rutting, defecating animal, and that the concept of faith will only blind him to the dreaded thing that is absolutely making its way to him. I want to tell him that if there is a God, he created death and dog shit and dementia. I want to tell him that God will abandon him, sometime, absolutely, and not to come running to me with any crap about how He works in mysterious ways.

I want to tell the man that the same sun that warms him and his nation of babies will burn him up; the same sun that looks down and sees his happiness sees unspeakable calamity everywhere else, all the time.

My response to the man's assault is always the same: an almost invisible nod without eye contact, a little croaked good morning that I feel compelled by guilt and doubt to deliver, making me even angrier; but always when the man expresses his relentless enthusiasm I want to slap his face or spit at him—something I would never do, of course. But I wish I lived in a world that would sanction my doing so, a just world that regarded the man's insistence regarding my happiness as some kind of violence, a transgression, a legitimate slap-provoking and spit-summoning event.

But I'm dogged by guilt about the shouting man. Who else is he supposed to be? I know that one event followed another, in just the right order, to make the man who he is; I know that the man received ideas from very specific sources, weighted just so, to construct his idea of things. I invoke the Buddhist principle: This is this because that was that. So to try to feel sympathy and maybe even empathy for the man, and be relieved of my guilt, I try to imagine a history that would produce a man like him; in this way I could think of him as somebody who had been a pretty baby, an innocent wrecked by bad luck. I wonder what defining event, what holocaust looms so large in the man's history. An undescended testicle? An elaborate tic? Early obesity? Arrested sexual development?

A speech impediment?

As I was about to go back through the gate, a decorated veteran of my walk, my dog pulled me across the street to the shouting man, still standing in front of his house waiting to share the gospel of the beautiful day with anyone within earshot. As if by design, the dog vomited at the man's feet, producing further evidence of his enlightenment. I throw up on your beautiful day, the dog seemed to say, to provide a question.

The End of the World

It seemed as though everyone in the neighborhood drifted to my house when the earthquake happened, like pups to their mother. It was four o'clock in the morning. My dog stumbled to the living room in a stupor. The big woman on the other side of the fence came in and wouldn't meet my eyes. The shouting man came with his wife and three babies; either the rest of the nation of babies were killed in the earthquake, or I'd miscalculated their numbers. The rest came. I don't know why they came to me. I locked myself in the bathroom and looked at myself in the mirror by the light of a match, to try to see what they saw, why they might have chosen me to rescue them. All I saw was the abysmal passage of the day; wretched world history nested in my face. Maybe they think I'm their point man for trouble. Anyone can see that I study trouble.

The electricity was out. We all stood at the windows, in

various stages of undress, and looked out at nothing. Then we all sat in the dark; I sat on my couch between two stunned, naked babies. We sat silently, eyes unfocussed, our brains fulminating over hallucinated images of magma, drifting to inculcated reveries of hell, of fire from the boiling center of the earth licking out of cracks like little tongues and burning us up for our crimes. It's the only explanation that makes sense, if you cleave to the idea that, in a churning universe of figments, there is sense to be made at all.

Three

WELL-LIKED MEN

1

My best friend Robert and I spend a good deal of time together, more than the orthodox local code for friendships between men seems to suggest, so we've been told.

We're very alike; we're both big men, not very handsome in relation to the standard set by the men to be seen in the magazines at the supermarket; we have faces that look like rock piles, humped backs, and large, coarse hands that look like they get things done. Lumpenproles. We are what we are. But we hope the consummate sense of us is that we're well-liked men, and appear to be serious men of some gravity, that if a mushroom cloud appeared on the horizon, citizens on the street would naturally rush to us to be rescued.

We're working stiffs, but bookish by temperament. We read voraciously, we've been around a while, and we've come to know a thing or two. We don't hesitate to take an aggressive opinion about things, whenever there are opportunities, of which there are an abundance, given what appears to be the inherently appalling nature of men and their consequence— the alarming drift of world events.

"Read a book, for chrissake," or "Have a look at yourself in the mirror," we might say to a man puffing his little chest out, blustering, making trouble for everyone wherever he goes; or, for a languishing, heartbroken man, "Back in the saddle, buddy." Clichés, we confess, but we've learned that our physical presence and our mellifluous voices mean more than what is being said, form over content.

Someone once said if you listen to any man's story for long enough you'll burst into tears. We know how a man might come to behave badly; and we try to forgive him, and in so doing forgive ourselves for the lingering impulse to make a little mayhem, to join the pissing contest, the primitive, unholy urge to dominate tucked just beneath our sympathies.

2

The question of the amount of time Robert and I spend together seems to mean to other men that we're secret homosexuals; they tease us, provoke us, and insist that we're in denial, but it isn't so. We've cooked together, traveled together, nursed and counseled one another, slept in the same bed many times; but it just isn't so. We've thoroughly discussed the subject between ourselves; shrinking away from each other, our eyes down to avoid contact, we wander around the room slowly, casually picking up a small object—a cup, perhaps—and examine it as though the conversation isn't important enough to draw our attention away from something so interesting.

"Do you think…?" I might say.

"Hmm? What?"

"You know, what we talked about?"

"Oh. No. No, definitely no," Robert will respond.

"But…," I say.

"Mm," Robert will say, mumbling.

"I'm sorry, what?"

"No!"

We've thought it through together thoroughly, and we can't find it in ourselves. That sort of intimacy between men seems like a fistfight to us, two belligerent *yangs* without a *yin*, certainly interesting as a curiosity, but inconceivable to us. As I say, we have spent a great deal of time together in intimate circumstances, on road trips and in the gym, and I've seen him naked many times; I've used each opportunity to mine myself rigorously for the most subtle scrap of desire: I can't find it. One night in a motel room on one of our road trips, while on my way to the bathroom in the middle of the night, I saw that his penis, illuminated by the narrow shaft of neon light coming through the slit in the curtain, had found its way out of the fly of his pajama bottoms like a little nocturnal animal looking for food. He was in one of his oblivious death-sleeps, so I took the opportunity to tiptoe over to him and study it at length with the little penlight on my keychain. I stared at the thing and waited. Nothing. I didn't have hungry man-love fantasies, I didn't wonder what it might be like to touch it or kiss it, I didn't take postures or bluster around insisting on my masculinity. Just nothing, no response at all. In fact I thought it was a little on the ugly side; it looks like something lonely and broken, and makes me wonder what God might have had in mind. If this withered flap of flesh is the totem of a phallocentric world, it's no wonder nothing works very well and we're all so uneasy.

Although we never speak of it, how we come to touch is an uncomfortable question; we have received and traditional ways of touching, certainly—painful slaps on the back, a man's brutal handshake, playful but hard punches to the arm. A man taken by affection for another man will curse him. I think the barbarity of it all is so there is no mistaking a touch for a caress; if a man's touch lingers, the moment is electric, and questions ensue.

Here and there we will inevitably need to pass each other in a tight space, a small doorway perhaps, and it's apparent that we're both aware of which pairing of body parts might imply something inappropriate, front to front, back to back, front to back. I dread the moments, and I sense that Robert does too. And in time, as a gesture of support or comfort in difficult times, at the news of a death, perhaps, we will inevitably be expected to hug, and I'm anxious about that, our privates looming in proximity like two little dogs straining at their leashes.

We've cried together, too—a very intimate thing to do, I think, when we come upon evidence of unredeemed heartbreak, of the anguish of an innocent child, or of an event so utterly without goodwill and kindness that all there is to do is cry. And I don't mean a little tear, or a quivering lip; I mean bawling, thrashing like little boys, snot flying, gasping sobs, knuckles in the eyeballs. And then, snuffling with puffy faces and stained cheeks, deepening our intimacy, we laugh at our own spectacle. We offer each other tissues and soft pats on the shoulder. How we must look.

So when our acquaintances gang up, giggle like stupid children and suggest that we're homosexuals, we tell them that of course we would face our nature squarely if it were indeed the case; but in this life it is not to be, we are what we are, and that is straight, like an arrow. For one, Robert has a wonderful wife. At least I assume she's wonderful, because knowing him as I do I can't imagine that he would be attracted to someone less so; but I don't know her at all, she's very aloof, she greets me formally and then pays little attention to me. She's tall and refined, graceful, and apparently very intelligent, traits from which I tend to shrink, and I take her reception of me badly. She might think I'm Robert's homosexual lover; everyone else does, why wouldn't she? Or, although she appears to ignore our conversations, I think she might be listening secretly and thinks what I have to say is ridiculous. I think I can see that she is very still and her eyes unfocus as she busies herself, paying no attention—sure signs that she is indeed listening. How could she not listen?

She makes me nervous; I confess to a discomfort regarding any third party lingering too close to the sovereign nation of Robert and me, and as his wife she looms large. I can't help but keep her in my peripheral vision when we're all in a room together, a kind of vigilance, as if she'll suddenly turn on me and humiliate me or strike me. It's all I can think about when she's nearby.

Then again, if I'm in a rare mood to be kind to myself, I allow the possibility that she might be attracted to me. I'm almost a twin to Robert in every way, in our looks and our temperament, even in our clothing; why wouldn't she find me generally attractive? It isn't unheard of that a woman might be resentful of a man to whom she's attracted and will treat him badly, ignoring him or glaring at him or being abrupt with him, anticipating the ordeal of pursuit and rejection, all the butterflies and swoons and agonies and sobs and at last heartbreak that will naturally eventuate from such a thing. Regarding her distance, it isn't unthinkable that she might be paralyzed with those inappropriate and contradictory feelings when I enter the room, and so appears aloof, which I misread as disinterest. I wonder if she keeps me in her peripheral vision the way I keep her in mine, looking for evidence, squirming, or a blush. I've allowed myself the cinematic fantasy of finding ourselves alone and suddenly throwing our bodies at one another for lacerating first kisses and gropes. I would never do this, of course; Robert is my dearest friend, my brother, my devotion.

Finally she's a kind of cardboard figure, an appendage oddly peripheral to our relationship. I don't like thinking about her; it seems inappropriate to think of her as a woman while she's the wife of my dear friend. I try not to think about her name, *Virginia*, so resonant with sexuality, and I try not to look at her body or be aware of her scent when she's nearby. Robert and I never talk about her, leaving certain questions of propriety unanswered, certain complexities untested, which is a source of some discomfort; given our intimacy, it doesn't feel good that something mustn't be talked about.

In sum, however these things work, from whatever wellspring, regarding our predispositions we appear to be the standard measure of the heterosexual male; Robert has this wife, to whom he is devoted, and I, myself, have an evolved enthusiasm, a *jones*, if you will, for women; I like all women for the simple reason of their womanness. I regard each and every woman I encounter—young and old, plain and beautiful, lumpy or sylphlike—and wonder about them. A woman's laugh, no matter how loud or coarse or foolish, will disarm me; I'm undone by a giggle. Ignorance, an errant hair, vulgarity, crossed eyes, a mustache will not disappoint.

On the street when we encounter men that know us, with a loud bark or giggling stupidly they're likely to throw a faux punch toward our stomachs, the greeting that we believe is the lingua franca of men in denial about their sexual preference. We believe they are sublimating their desire to kiss us or fondle us; we jump back, to suggest that a love-punch is inappropriate and will hurt just as much as a malevolent one, and say, "A simple hello and a wave will do, don't you think?" We say it with friendly smiles and an avuncular tone, because we make it our business to be sympathetic to the bad behavior of every man, given the certainty that when they were small boys they received their life lessons from the same ignorant mentors that gave us ours. But it is so clear that *they're* the ones who may be suppressing their homosexual feelings, and we later confess to one another that their hypocrisy makes us want to punch *them* in the stomach.

We laugh, but affectionately, thinking about them in front of their full-length mirrors before they hit the street, posturing, making threat-faces, trying for authority. We know these men were once sweet babies and good little boys; but when a man on the street looks at me with that moldering expression, or when a man greets me and squeezes my hand so hard I get little tears in my eyes, or delivers a stinging slap on the back, or curses me to compensate for his repressed love-feelings, I have to confess that before I can position myself as sympathetic or empathetic, I have fast hot fantasies of punching his lights out and standing over his inert body shouting—which I would never do, of course. But for a moment the primitive brain swims up and eclipses good sense and propriety. Nevertheless I feel guilty; to compensate for the feelings of guilt that this kind of extreme fantasy inevitably produces, I always compulsively finish it with a redemptive hug, wherein a lesson is learned by both of us.

If all of this isn't evidence of our heterosexuality, then I don't know where else to look, or what else to say about the subject. It is what it is, enough said.

3

Every morning, Robert and I meet at our favorite little cafe. Our way: a croissant with savory jams, espresso in tiny cups, poignant in our big mitts, stubby pinkies akimbo, and we read the newspaper together, passing sections back and forth. Politically we tend to be sensitive to the plight of the exploited and oppressed, the underdog. We embrace our ruined and maligned brothers and sisters. Every story in the paper, every day, seems in some way to be about the boot of the oppressor on our backs; we root out a good story about injustice and comment with full voice in outrage. If all the other customers in the café are in our range, so be it; they will have been privileged to come upon the reckonings of two thoughtful men who read, who do their homework. We rage on into the morning. If one of us is feeling the fire, he may take postures and slip into a little speech-making while the other calls out a righteous *"Right on, bud!"* or *"Tell it!"* pounding the table decisively, beating out a rhythm for emphasis. Or, if we're deeply moved by a well-written story of catastrophe, in which there is no apparent perpetrator, we'll discuss the concept of fate or debate the existence of a higher power; but each time we finally shrug and intone: "Whaddaya gonna do?," Because what *are* you going to do? And we wag our heads slowly from side to side and sigh simultaneously, as if we'd rehearsed it.

4

"You know, that wife of yours is one fine woman."

We sat, early in the morning, at our usual table in the café. I had been lost in thought; I said this carelessly to myself but out loud. I could see in my peripheral vision that Robert had jerked his head up and was staring at me. I realized suddenly that I had addressed the subject of his wife for the first time, and that he had the same thought; the taboo had been established retroactively by the act of violating it. I watched him peripherally, watching me, both of us startled.

"Oh? And?"

We stared at each other.

"And nothing."

"What do you mean by 'one fine woman'?"

"What do you mean, what do I mean? She's a fine woman. That's it."

"But what do you mean? That she seems like a *nice* woman?"

"Exactly, yes."

"An interesting woman."

"Yes."

"Intelligent."

"Yes. Why are you asking me these questions?"

"A *good* woman, all around."

"Of course, yes."

He leaned in across the tiny table, closer to me; his big boulder of a chin jutted out like a cartoon. "What else?"

"What do you mean, what else? Nothing else. I can't think of anything else."

"Do you like the way she looks?"

"Of course I do. She's very attractive."

He leaned in closer, looking very threatening; his eyes were slits, and the little punctum of light in his pupils pierced like a laser. My back was against the wall; by instinct I put my hands on my chest protectively.

"Attractive? What do you mean, 'attractive'? Attractive how?"

"What's wrong with you? I'm telling you I think your wife is a beautiful woman."

"Oh, *beautiful*? Not *attractive* anymore?"

"Well, frankly, I regret using the word beautiful. I'm afraid it might sound as if I was thinking about her inappropriately."

He stared at me.

"So you consciously wrestled with the thought? You think my wife is beautiful, but you think I might not like it if you said so, so you say she's *attractive*? You've developed a strategy to keep inappropriate thoughts at bay?"

"I suppose you could say that."

"Sexual thoughts?"

"Well, I suppose, yes."

"You repress your sexual thoughts."

"I suppose you could say it that way too."

"Do you repress sexual thoughts about my wife?"

"What do you mean?"

"It's a simple question. Yes or no. Do you?"

"How can a person know if he's repressing a thought?"

He stared at me.

"Well, do you *think* you do?"

I stared back.

"Alright, even though I wouldn't know it consciously, because the thoughts would be repressed, as a student of men's foibles I'd have to say yes, I probably do, but unconsciously. That's the way the mind works, no? But if the thought is unconscious, no transgression is committed, because I wouldn't even know I was thinking it."

He loomed even closer. He lowered his voice to a purr.

"Don't you mean *sub*consciously?" He narrowed his eyes in

a leer to suggest that my swinish, predatory self was closer to the surface of consciousness than I was willing to admit.

"Alright, *sub*consciously. But still, not conscious, so no transgression is committed."

Robert stared at me unblinking, close, his eyes eating into me, through skin and bone, through the dura mater, through the cerebral cortex, mining the layers of rational, socialized thought to find the monkey brain that would hump the wife of its best friend.

"But you'd have to give it *some* conscious thought to conclude that she's a 'good woman,' to make a judgment of any kind, wouldn't you? You think of a scale, from a bad woman to a good woman, let's say, or from a plain woman to a beautiful one, and you make a judgment. You're at home, alone with your private thoughts, which can take any form because they're unexpressed, no social or moral issues to consider— therefore yours to have for your own amusement. The thought of my wife occurs for no particular reason, maybe you think of her doing some common thing, like crossing a room. You get a visual picture and suddenly you think about her dress flowing back and forth with the movement, swirling around her pretty legs, maybe you think about her breasts heaving, maybe the light is beautiful in your thought, and there it is: Oh, of course, this is a *woman*, regardless of the fact that she's my best friend's wife, it never occurred to me before, this is a *woman*. And then, what sort of woman might this be, is she beautiful or not, a common thought by a man regarding a woman, and you conclude that, yes indeed, she *is* beautiful."

He was thorough; he'd set a linguistic trap for me. I couldn't deny what he was saying.

"I suppose that could happen. But . . . ,"

"So. You have her in your head, in your fantasy. The thought of her is in your head, and you're free to do anything you want to her there, because you're the sole author and audience of your unexpressed thoughts. You can do things to her and then have her say, breathlessly, oh, my god, thank you, you're the best, better than my clumsy dimwit of a husband, I had no idea it could be like this. You could have a giant horse penis and I could have a little pee-pee in your fantasy. You can dress me like a fool or a little boy. You could be doing things to her right *now*, for chrissake. While you're sitting here, looking me right in the eye. While I'm talking to you, you could be serving it up to her, humping the stuffing out of her, and I'm watching, holding your underpants, dressed like a *little boy*!"

"What's wrong with you?"

"Isn't this true in potential, at least?"

"I'd have to agree that it's true in potential, yes. But it's just a polemical agreement."

"Do you?"

He was glaring, an inch from my face by now. I felt his breath on me; I thought of a lizard sniffing me to determine if I was food.

"Do I what?"

"Do you do things to my wife in your fantasies?"

"*No.* No. Absolutely not."

"Oh? My wife, who you regard as a beautiful woman? She isn't sexual? She has no vagina in your fantasies? No breasts? No nipples?"

"What?"

"Does she have a vagina?"

"Yes, for god's sake, I'm sure she has one, but it's hidden, it's not for me to see or think about or know about, just like in real life. Or it's just neutral, the way a doctor might think about it."

"But you think about the fact of its being hidden. Therefore you think about it."

"I suppose you can make a deductive case that if I think about your wife in my head, all of her parts are necessarily included in the thought of her."

"So today, in this moment, you, my best friend in the world, are telling me that you think about my wife's vagina."

I moaned, dropping my head into my hands.

"*Do* you? *Do* you?"

A little spit flew from the hard consonant D.

"Yes! I guess so! *Christ!*"

We sat in silence; my head hung as if my neck were broken. Robert's head was almost touching mine; he lowered it and squinted into my pupils, as if he might be able to look through them to the usurped image of his wife's vagina hanging like a chandelier inside my eyeballs. He made fists that looked like roasts. I realized I was leaning away from him at an unnatural angle and my body ached. At last he straightened, his fists opened slowly, he sat quietly in thought for a time, and finally spoke.

"I don't know what to do. One part of me wants to slap you in the face for thinking about my wife in that way. But another part of me is moved; my wife *is* beautiful, and if you didn't think so, I'd probably be upset. I don't know what to do."

I sighed and reflected.

"I don't know what to do either. One part of me feels guilty for thinking about her that way. Another part of me, though— forgive me, a very *little* part—if I think it through, a repressed, instinctive part—wants to slap *your* face, to dominate you; I want you to accept that I'm a man, your dearest friend but a man after all, and you and I know more than anyone, given our discussions, that men are likely to have a cheap or carnal thought about any woman who has the bad luck to come into their sights, any woman, your best friend's woman notwithstanding. It's natural for a man to have a thought like this. That's not unthinkable, is it?"

We sat silently for a long time. Occasionally one or the other would cry out, "I don't know what to do!"

Finally, overwhelmed and exhausted by the painful conversation, we fell asleep at the little table.

We awoke at the same moment. We rubbed our eyes, looked up at each other startled, and at the same moment lunged across the table and slapped each other in the face as hard as we could. We struck with such perfect simultaneity that it produced a single sharp sound.

Four

The Betty

1

I had a wife once. We lived together in my tiny cottage at The Betty. She was a good wife, attentive and sweet. Whenever I settled into my chaise lounge on the little square of gleaming grass in front of our cottage, I kept sitting up and craning my neck back to see her moving among our carefully chosen things, our furniture and artwork, framed by the picture window. This is good, this is good, I'd say to myself while I watched her; a man who has conjured this spectacle must be a very clever and attractive one, this is good,

Amen. The courtyard is a communal area, but sometimes the thought loomed so large I laughed out loud, and the other residents of the Betty, who always look as if they had died on their own chaise lounges, sat up startled.

One day while I lay there my wife called my name from the doorway of the cottage; I sat up and turned back to see her in my usual aroused way. In an indifferent voice, she called out that she was tired of me, and left, right then, right out the door, past me, and down the path to the sidewalk. She turned North, toward the colder climate.

I lay there well into the night. I won't ever move again, I thought, I'll just dry up here, languish, and crack to atoms.

It is a terrible thing to be abandoned because someone is tired of you. How do I tell the story without whining and begging kindness for a man so tedious, so without appeal, that even his loved ones wander away from him without a good explanation? No one has sympathy for the fool left in this way; they don't want to see it.

No one at The Betty has ever asked me a thing about it. But if they do, I've decided to make up a story, and I plan to be very attractive in it—because why would I want to tell them a story in which I'm a minnow of a man?

2

I can see directly across the courtyard into the picture window of the little German man and his very large wife and their pale, haunted daughter. They're new to The Betty and I haven't met them yet. I'm very aware of them, but I'm much too bashful to introduce myself; I'll fall down and hurt myself on my way over to them, or accidentally spit on them when I speak. Certainly my voice will catch and I'll gag or squeal. To ask me to march across the lawns like The Man Who Gets Things Done and stick my hand out is asking just too much. The small, finite square of grass between us is an infinite emergency to me.

My cottage is identical to theirs, and our stuffed armchairs just inside our picture windows are so similar that sometimes when the German and I both sit there and read, I look up over my book and think for an instant that I'm looking at my reflection. The untended grapefruit tree is between us, and from my perspective, rotting fruits hang around his image like moldering brains. I'm not much for omens or symbolism; I like hard ground. But I can't not think about it—this spectacle colors my idea of the man, as if I'm looking at a sinister version of myself. I can't help it, and it makes me suspicious of him.

Meeting him is inevitable, though, unless by an accident of good luck we all die of natural causes before the event.

I was told by the unreadable old Slavic man who lives in the cottage next door to them that the German is difficult. I'm very uncomfortable around unreadable men, and especially foreign men, because I can never be certain that we're talking about the same thing. But I plan to approach the old man sometime and ask him just what the German did to make him think he's so difficult. As I say, I'm not an abstract or poetic kind of thinker, but I can't help the thought that the rotting fruit is a sign, put there by Providence before the man's image to settle the question about the nature of his character. And that is very bad news to me, because when there is a man close by who has any kind of questionable reputation, I think about him too much and I feel the need to keep a lookout for him, a kind of vigil, which is exhausting. For me there seems to be a man like this wherever I go, in every setting. I study them as if I were looking through a telescope at a meteorite and plotting its course right to the center of my forehead.

Next door to the German man, the unreadable old Slav can always be seen lying on his lounge squarely in front of his door in a proprietary way. There is a wife; she is never seen, but I think she's right behind him, inside, a foot from him as he lies there, on her own chair hidden behind the screen door. I imagine her as skeletal, perhaps fingering catechism beads, muttering devotions, or whispering endearments or curses to her husband through the screen door. Two skinny, lavender-white legs poke out of the old man's enormous camouflage shorts. His conceit is a shiny silver pompadour that he attends to regularly, there on the lounge, spraying it, patting it, propping it up.

The old man is inert; if he thinks, or has feelings, nothing of it reaches the surface. I'm jealous of him, too; in relation to him I must seem like a hysterical and public fool.

I think about the man. Once when I was a boy, my father

came to my bedroom, took me by the hand, and brought me to the big mirror in the living room. We regarded ourselves. It's time to talk about being a man, he said. His concept, which he said he had learned from *his* father, was that if I look intelligent and keep my mouth shut, I'll be seen as a self-possessed man, and that will intimidate another man, whose bad luck it will be to pass me in the streets that day; he'll be sure I'm thinking about *him*, and that he doesn't measure up. You'll see his shoulders drop, my father said; this is submission, the kick-me position, and you'll be the champ of the moment. Trust me, he said, a man secretly wants to knuckle under to another man's authority; he isn't happy until he finds his place, even if he finds out that his place is to be second-rate, where he belongs, where it's okay to be mediocre, where he doesn't have to exhaust himself being number one. That's how it works, he said. He furrowed his brow and pointed to the furrow. Make your forehead like this, he said. We both turned and looked in the big mirror and furrowed. Good, he said, now just shut up, and you have it.

The old Slav is good at it, his ridiculous spectacle notwithstanding. He seems absolutely impenetrable; he can see what's up while I invent conundrums and the world slips and slides. Or so I think; maybe the man is just an idiot, maybe he isn't thinking about anything at all. But I'm jealous of that, too; how blissful it would be to lie on my chaise lounge with a full stomach and think about nothing, to feel the sun on me until something else happens.

I have an impulse to test the old man, to run across the courtyard and spit at him or pull his hair to see just how self-possessed he really is. Of course I'd never do such a thing, but oh, if only.

3

The German man's wife is very large, to the point of being a curiosity. When I first saw her I studied her; I sat in the darkened front room of my cottage and looked at her through my picture window the way a man looks at the Statue of Liberty. I began to think of her as a kind of Erda, a stupendous Wagnerian earth goddess. Everything about her is abundant and moves autonomously; when she comes out onto the lawn through the front door of her cottage it looks like fruits, candies, and roasts tumbling out of a cornucopia onto the gleaming grass. She's a good-looking woman—handsome, specifically—anyone would think so. But I hadn't given it much thought until one day when I heard her laugh; its gurgling little sing-song made me suddenly aware that she was, in fact, a woman, replete with a woman's plums and pearls, and the thought shot a beam right through to my monkey brain, which knows nothing about good sense or propriety. The world was new. The next morning I pushed my armchair farther back into the shadows of my front room and waited for her to come out, so I could continue to study her.

Soon I started to have sexual fantasies about her. I don't

know why; I don't generally take to large women. As my fantasies deepened and got more elaborate I tried to add love scenes to the sexual narratives, but it was no use. She's too big; I'd have to stand on a stool to take the traditional position for kisses, to swallow her into my embrace.

Although she's too big for romantic love, and I'm afraid of her husband, I take the risk of watching her whenever I can, lying on my chaise lounge pretending I'm reading or asleep, or crossing my little patch of grass to pluck a weed, for cover. I bought very dark sunglasses so I can appear to be looking at something else while I'm really looking at her.

In my fantasies I imagine stirring after a dreamless sleep with her, then crawling over the vast landscape of her body, occasionally stopping to shout a *Hosanna!* for my good luck, making my way through her sweetmeats and nooks, her crannies and confections, over the milky hills and darkling perfumed valleys of her Bunyanesque thighs while, as Erda, she sings, "*Stark ruft das Lied! Kraftig reizt der Zauber!*" "*Strong is your call! Mighty spells have roused me!*"

Foolish, maybe, but in my fantasies I'm God Almighty, and if, in them, I want her to sing an aria while I have her, or if I want to include the husband in them—have him, say, clean my apartment or hold my things while I make his wife yodel—it's my own business, isn't it? Where else in this suffocating shit life can I have things just the way I want them? I'm president of all of my fantasies, and if I assign somebody a role in one, they might be forewarned that in them I'm sovereign, sole author of the story, and they might be asked to do something disagreeable.

But I'm afraid of the woman, because I'm certain that to have anything to do with her threatens to draw me into a confrontation with her husband, who has already aroused suspicion as a man who won't have my well-being in mind. As is my way, the way of anticipating absolute ruin in every endeavor big and small, in every clime and on every land mass and body of water I traverse, in this life and the next, I think the man will somehow find out I have inappropriate thoughts about his wife. He'll go berserk and suddenly run across the little lawns and gardens at me, crushing the flowers, to humiliate me or hurt me grievously.

Once on the TV news I saw an interview with a man who, during a public beating by a stranger, had his eye punched out, his spleen ruptured, and his front tooth knocked out; he was so clever with language, so poetic and vivid in his description of the beating that as I watched and listened I grunted and screamed and cried as if *I* were being beaten. In all my fantasies of confrontation since then, these three stigmata have become the features of my undoing; and if the German man attacks me, I know this will be the result.

Even the sad, silent daughter looms as a threat; I've conjured a story about her in which she is in denial about an appalling event in the past, one that has sapped her; one day it will suddenly make itself known in some way, she'll go berserk, kill her parents and come for me next, right down the beaten path through the flower beds that her father made. Although she's small and sallow, her colossal rage will make her able to overwhelm me.

This is my way; I'm afraid of them, and by degree everyone and everything in the world. Fear is my general organizing principle, my way.

When I was a little boy my mother and aunts took me to the park in my massive velveteen and chromed carriage, pulled me gasping and sweating from my silken goose down blankets and monogrammed, embroidered pillows and tried to put me on the tootle train. I had a strong premonition of catastrophe; I clutched my mother's hem with both fists and refused to board. Absolutely the tootle train would derail, throw me, and crush me. Vividly I saw my tiny baby feet sticking out from beneath it, the toes perfect, unblemished baby jewels; I experienced a lavish wave of self-pity that was so ecstatic I fell in love with myself right then, deeply.

It was a defining moment; since then I'm certain that anything might rise up out of the ether to hurt me: a careening car, a tumor exploding in my cerebral cortex or eating my lung. A bullet meant for someone else might pass through me on its way. Maybe a dangerous lunatic, born a long time ago and far away, is making his way to *me*, given the random happenstances of a life. Why isn't everybody as nervous as me about what's rushing blindly toward *them*? Even as a small boy at the tootle train I concluded that we're no more than a flap of flesh, a nervous and palsied thing in an inconsolable,

anarchic universe, and all we can do is to try to find a safe
route through the chaos, through the day. Attendant is the
wonderful and heady cocktail of self-love and self-pity. I used
to try to discuss this idea with acquaintances, but I learned
that if I wanted to have acquaintances at all, I'd better keep it
to myself.

I cried my eyes out for the rest of that day, during milk
time, during nap time, loudly at the swings, which also looked
fatally dangerous to me, back and forth, back and forth, back
and forth to no purpose. I bawled at the water fountain,
puled at the ice cream truck, and ululated in the port-a-potty,
everywhere shaking and weeping, big beamy tears splashing,
causing my lips to swell and redden like shiny cherries and my
big, limpid dark brown eyes and long black lashes to glisten,
an enchanting picture to my mother and aunts, even to the
other mothers, whose babies had boarded the train stupidly
like lambs in an abattoir; they gathered around and loomed
over me, grabbing and pawing. Poor baby, poor baby, they
said, look at that face. I looked through the mist of my tears
from one beefy shadow to another, immense, supple, lactating
mothers of all of us and even of God, then to each of the
other babies, riding the tootle train oblivious and unwitnessed
in a circle that went nowhere. So, hmm . . . I thought, by the
beauty and eloquence of my grief I had usurped all the fleshy
wonderments, all the fluvial, milky mothers to myself, as far
as the eye could see; the other babies will grow hungry and
languish as they go around and around slowly to no discernible

purpose and wonder dimly, with too few developed synapses to adequately presage the future, what was going to happen to them given the alarming implications of an infinite circle. It seemed to me even then to be a sure recipe for melancholy, which would bloom frighteningly later in their lives. The mothers wiped my nose and stroked my head, cooed and cupped my hot cheeks with their fat palms and tugged on my earlobes and radiated dizzy love at me. I smelled them and leaned into their ministrations like a blade of grass to the sun. I knew then that I had a plan: Being inconsolable would be my way of moving through the world powerfully and safely. We're all the way we are because of just exactly what happened to us, in the way that it did, aren't we? Everyone has a plan, don't they? This is mine.

4

Today the German man suddenly looked up from his reading and caught me looking at his wife. He stood up and stared at me for a long time through his picture window. I panicked; I jumped off the lounge to my feet and looked around frantically as if I had lost something, so it would seem to them that the look was an accident. When he caught me, I was having a fantasy of being held in a headlock by her, smothered between bosoms and bellies; guilt and fear caused me to think that the husband had somehow been able to see this image, in perfect detail, as if I had a thought balloon above my head. Now the German will come and attack me in a fit of jealous rage, and at his trial, head down and weeping quietly, he'll describe the humiliation and heartbreak of my crime so poignantly that the jury will find him not guilty for beating me, after which all the chaste and virtuous people in the courtroom will turn to me as one, with an indignant eye. I'll stumble around The Betty for the rest of my life, half blind, without a front tooth or a spleen, anathema to the smug residents, for whom I will be an object lesson in the failure of propriety.

The German came out of his cottage and began to walk toward me, purpose in his stride. It seemed to take him a thousand years to reach me; I thought about suddenly running *toward* him, shouting a confession: "*But she doesn't love me!*" I'd shout as I ran, right into his arms. "*I'm sure she loves only you!*" I thought about running right out of the courtyard and down the street with only the clothes on my back to another city where I'd make a new life, perhaps to the North where I might spy my wife. But I stood, a condemned man paralyzed in the German's thrall, waiting for the blow.

I knew he was smallish, but as he got closer I realized he was a little jewel of a man, tiny and meticulous with a razor-sharp part in his gleaming black hair, small enough to be an oddity among the lawn chairs, which gave him scale. He was well proportioned and conventionally handsome, a perfect miniature; very delicate, pink, translucent skin, scrubbed immaculately. He really *is* tiny, I thought, a neat little homunculus. As he approached he held my eyes; I gaped stupidly back at him until I was able to will myself to look away. I fixated on the part in his hair, on its perfection; in my mind I saw his colossal wife fussing with it, being a kind of curator of his part. I stifled the urge to laugh. He put a hand out to be shaken, and I took it. I looked down at his tiny hand swimming in my relatively immense palm, and the impulse to laugh bloomed alarmingly; to keep from exploding in his face I tried to remember painful moments from my past—lost love, a holocaust, the death of a puppy.

"My wife, Ilsa, and I, and our daughter, Imke, would like to introduce ourselves," he said with a slight German accent, while squeezing my big hand with his little one so hard that tears came to my eyes.

I looked up and Ilsa and Imke smiled and waved a greeting like synchronized swimmers.

5

In the warm season, the residents of The Betty lie outside the doorways of their little cottages like potentates of tiny territories on fabulous, throne-like chaise lounges with floral patterns and fringes and cup holes embedded in the arms. There seems to be an uneasy entente among the residents; they're polite but suspicious and rarely speak to each other, acknowledging each other's presence from their little principalities with curt nods and little hand waves. The grass gleams around them.

Ilsa lies on her lounge like a receding landscape of mountain ranges; from my perspective I see her feet first, then knees, then bellies, then breasts topped by burly nipples, her nose visually between them, and finally her gleaming blue-black bouffant. Dreamily I imagine an event: I shimmy up her legs, pause for a moment of pious silence at her holy of holies, scrabble up her bellies and slide down to the foothills of her breasts. I stop there; I have no interest in the thing that resides in her face. I don't kiss her; my kisses are only for love, and I don't love her. The frail, wan daughter lies next to her on her child-size lounge and burns up in the sun. The tiny husband stays at his post in the window and comes out occasionally to see if they're comfortable and brings them drinks, which he offers smartly, like a waiter. Since he introduced himself to me, I can look in their direction and think about having sex with his wife while greeting him with a neighbor's wave and smile. I enjoy even more disgraceful sex fantasies about his wife while I smile at him, not because I'm mean-spirited but simply to establish and insist that I am the sole author and audience of my thoughts, Amen.

But there's been a development; I think Ilsa might be looking at *me* in her peripheral vision; her eyes seem to lose focus and she holds her head very still, they way I do when I'm angling a look at her. This has caused me to think about how I look, a conundrum because I have grave doubts in that area in general: my ears stick out like cup handles; my nose is too long; and I think the depth of attention I pay to things makes me look a little cross-eyed. Some women have found these to be attractive features, but that is a good example of how utterly confounded I am about how a woman might like me to be. In any event I have no pointers about what kind of man Ilsa might find attractive, other than that she might be desiring of a man larger than the tiny German.

But I've learned from studying my reflection in the German's window that the light of the late afternoon makes me look best; for a little while in this season the arc of the sun brings out a handsome groove in my cheek if I hold my head a certain way. In the magazines at the supermarket, every public man who is regarded as handsome has this feature. Also, when I lie on the chaise lounge I try to compose my body in the languid and graceful position of a thinking man, which I've been told is attractive to a woman; while other men flee, fight, do the work, I will do the thinking. On the other hand, not knowing her I can't decide if I should try to look graceful or vulgar. Some women like vulgar and difficult men, I've heard, to be thrummeled on dirty sheets—God bless them.

6

I returned from a trip out of town to learn that while I was away the German man had died. The daughter is gone. I crossed the little squares of grass to the old Slav, who explained to me that the man had choked on a piece of chicken served

to him on a paper plate by Ilsa while he lay on his chaise
lounge, and was dead in a minute. He delivered his report in a
monotone, expressionless. I could not help but have an image
of Ilsa, perhaps desiring of a larger man, watching the man
dispassionately as he turned purple and passed.

He said the daughter was not Ilsa's, and that she'd gone to
live with her real mother. As usual, at the news of a death I felt
nothing but the discomfort of being examined and critiqued
for my performance of grief. When I was a boy and my
grandmother died, I spent a whole day hidden in the bathroom,
in front of the mirror practicing a response to the inevitable
expectation that I say something regarding her death; using a
hand mirror to study my profiles, again and again I hung my
head, knitted my brows, mumbled something, and shook my
head slowly like a bell tolling. That seemed best to me. Now,
with the old Slav as my witness, I forced my body to suggest
that the German's death was a great loss to us all. But all I
could think of was that Ilsa was in her cottage alone, and if
God loved me, I would make her cry out that very night. It
wouldn't be unthinkable that I would look toward their cottage
as a gesture to the grieving widow, and I took the opportunity;
I saw her large silhouette moving deep inside and tried to
fight off images of love silhouettes, inappropriate under the
circumstance. I bowed my head to cover a dirty smirk, and
excused myself to go inside to ruminate about death and think
about the implications of Ilsa alone in her cottage without the
German and his daughter as impediments to my desire.

But as the days pass she doesn't come out of her cottage. Her picture window is like a movie screen to me, and from behind my window, deep in my own darkened front room, I watch her simple daily routines. The rotted, brain-like fruits have fallen, and now in the warm season there are pretty, fragrant blossoms, illuminating her image as the brains once spoiled her husband's. I'm developing what I think are rudimentary love feelings for her, and I'm in a torment. I tend to get lovesick, and I know that soon I could be in a swoon.

I can't stop thinking about her; now, without her family in the way, the spectral mothers of the tootle train incident are wound into this colossus of a woman. While all the other babies on the train were abandoned to survive an infinite circle of meaningless events, I stood among their purloined mothers, exultant and smug, denied a lesson of survival; I know now that this is the calculus of my crippling. Now, as I punish myself, all the toughened and savvy babies are somewhere in the city, grown up and sitting with their families, with full stomachs, in front of the television. Their families are beautiful, and they all laugh at the same time and treat each other to smiles and sweets and endearments, while I regard the large woman as if I were looking through a telescope at a remote planet.

I think about crossing the gardens to make a consolation visit but I know I'll just gape at her, or start to laugh inexplicably, or try to make love to her, and then I'll try but I won't be able to explain any of it, why love eclipses good sense and propriety.

So I do nothing. I console myself with the fact that she's so large I won't be able to get my arms all the way around her. I'll feel like a boy when she bends down to me for my kisses. When I lie on my chaise lounge I'll stare at her immense underpants hanging on the clothesline. Maybe she has a mean streak. Maybe she's a drunk, or can't read, or suffers from a mental illness. I don't even know if she speaks English.

At best she looks out with different eyes into a world unrecognizable to me, lurid in its bizarre approximation of mine.

Weeks have gone by. As I move about my day I watch her through her picture window the way I once watched my wife. I can see her television, and I watch it with her; I can't hear her or the TV but I can see her laugh and cry as she watches it, and so I laugh and cry with her. I invent conversations, in which I'm always very clever, in which she gapes at me while I declaim. I go to bed when she does, and in my reveries about her before I fall sleep, given that I am President and Prime Minister of all my fantasies, she's tiny, and she loves me like crazy, and I overwhelm her completely with my kisses.

Five

❧

THE ROYAL JELLY

Whenever the woman enters the seminar rooms, I turn away, while the rest of the associates watch her obliquely, or directly if they can find a reason. I turn away formally, even theatrically, to execute a willful snub, my nose in the air, announcing that I refuse to be engaged by her spectacle. I study the other men, watching them watch her; they look at her the way a man looks at the Statue of Liberty, or a painting of the Virgin Mary. They all think about having sex with her, and they're aroused; they're preening, composing themselves as handsomely as they know how to find their way to her.

But they're uneasy. They're accomplished and vain men; they know if they fail it will be a heavy blow to their conceit, and if they succeed it will be a difficult pilgrimage, and absolutely finite.

Everyone thinks of the woman as beautiful, but she is *lovely*, specifically, and as a result some of the men might also be having love fantasies, ones that include kissing and endearments. But they have crude, carnal thoughts about her, too, and this contradiction makes them even more restless and unhappy.

There are rules at the Institute, ones that make sense, given the strain of the people here. One rule high on the list is that sexual contact between the associates is forbidden. Cosmologies are a good part of my field of study, and even though I'm not an institute sort of person, I think I can see what the administration had in mind when they designed rules specifically to keep these fragile and inconsolable people out of trouble. In sum, if one associate has sex with another, it will disturb the carefully woven web of associations necessary to do the kind of byzantine, esoteric work that's done here, and I completely agree. It isn't easy to maintain stability in this small group of delicate, easily unsettled wizards.

Now the associates are at a pitch. Months have passed since her arrival, and no one has succeeded in having sex with her. She pays no attention to them. She doesn't make eye contact or greet anyone or have conversations. They can't help themselves; they keep her in their peripheral vision as they circumnavigate her unhappily, sighing like boys. Every day she eats alone in the cafeteria and I watch them orbiting with their trays, trying to land close to her, trying to calculate the right arc and the right words to cross the colossal gap between them and their spectral dream. Then an endearing disappointment on their faces when they lose the rhythm or the will and miss the point of entry. They eat alone at tiny tables like punished children.

They're all erudite men, posturing men by trade, but when they get too close to her, they wiggle like irritable babies. They make jerky movements. They laugh like barking dogs, they giggle and squeal, and if these are men who habitually think very carefully about what they say, when she's nearby they don't think at all. They're out of control; they're losing the carefully manicured persona evolved over decades.

She is the locus of too much attention, and it shakes the Institute. Something is going to happen.

I've read her work. In her field, it turns everything on its head, sending percussion waves everywhere; like her, the arguments are beautiful and unsettling. And I also agree that she is truly lovely. A startling and fragile blossom. The Royal Jelly. But I refuse to submit like the other associates. I'm very busy, and I have a more evolved and more cerebral notion of love and relations. I don't—I won't—want this woman. I'm resolved to not want this woman.

This morning in the men's room the associates were lined

up at the urinals shoulder to shoulder. Someone had written her name on the wall above the center urinal, and each day for five days someone added a carefully drawn heart, in pencil, one for each day at each corner of her name, and finally one larger heart above the rest, with little flames licking around the edges: Burning Love Ascendant and Triumphant. As we stood we leaned in and studied the images. I examined the rendered hearts; I concluded that a man who renders a heart so carefully must love the woman named. One of us is in love, and we all wonder who it might be, who might walk the path before us.

We mused. One of the associates, our semiotician, suggested that the suit she wore to seminars, along with her glasses, was the costume of a woman in thrall to the love arts. He was silent as the rest of us brooded on his theory.

Yes! he shouted, and gave himself a more vigorous final shake than usual. The men whooped and high-fived down the line. I knew it wasn't this associate who was in love; no man would say such an offensive and dismissive thing about someone they loved. I lost my temper; *What's wrong with you?* I asked him, as I heard the terms of my own undoing, as if the man were my own libido and had leaped out of my body horned and red-faced and bleating like a goat. *Do you hear yourself? You sound like an idiot!* Manic and grinning, he threw a fake punch at my stomach, the lingua franca of men who repress their natural desire to give another man a beating. This drew more guttural whoops from the men.

This is the sort of language and behavior that has taken hold among these polished and articulate men, and I don't like it. I'll stick with my standard pose: I walk down the halls of the Institute slowly with my head down, my hand on my chest or my chin, with as much gravitas as I can summon up, suggesting with my body language that I'm primarily a cerebral man, that the sad, finite, and putrefactive corpus exists only to cogitate on the meaning of its minim of sentient being. I'm a vehicle for the intellect, not an oaf swinging his penis, like this associate. Shouting Hosannas to God for His Good Grace as I Die of Bliss in the Arms of the Loveliest Woman on Earth will have to wait while I'm thinking about the impenetrable conundrums characteristic of my specialty.

She is a Germanist. "*Ach. Es geht mir schlecht in Berlin,*" she sighs at a meeting, presumably to begin a story. She is alarmingly pale, small in the big chair. She can make her fragile body look like it's broken, and all of the associates' hearts break simultaneously. *There is only entropy*, she tells us with her posture. *Let's all kill ourselves*, she pantomimes.

I watched them watching her as she spoke. They were trying to learn. She hasn't responded to their ebullience and charm, and her intellectual accomplishments outdo theirs absolutely; so now they appeared to be trying out their most existential expressions and postures to try to ingratiate themselves to her, to suggest that they're fellow travelers, that like her they're also world-weary and emotionally bankrupt—that believing life has a purpose is ludicrous. They've closed the collars of their shirts, and they've stooped a little, walking with their heads down as if in thought, presumably to signify that they've been around a while, that they know something—that like her, they've been beaten by life. We look into the same abyss, they try to say with their postures. But they aren't good at this pose, being fundamentally lively and highly engaged men, so they all look only as if they don't feel well. I suddenly realized that my rehearsed and polished gravitas would be misunderstood by her in the context of their poses; that I might seem to her to be one of them. I had a sudden urge to jump up and shout to her that I am most definitely *not* one of them. Of course I didn't do it, but I took the thought as evidence that I'm slipping.

With her posture and her comment in German—*I was down and out in Berlin*—she wants to tell us that she has had a depraved and failed life, that nihilism is finally the only critique of an unreasonable and godless world. Well done, I whispered to myself; I had to confess witnessing her craft was a pleasure for a man of my proclivities, which are—like hers I think—to try to be artful and circumspect as I move through a room and to be very talented at knowing just what's going on in it.

She made her comment in German. *Bear-lean.* I'm a secular Talmudic scholar; I'm fluent in five living languages and three dead ones, and I knew very well what her words meant in English, but innocently I asked her to translate. I looked like a lost boy as I asked her; playing to someone's conceits is always a good strategy to inch closer to them. Everybody loves to tell you all about themselves, so I say make the holy space for them to do it, and then listen hard.

Also, a confession: If the truth be told, like the great chess masters who see their victory fifty moves ahead and stand up and walk out, I began to think at least subconsciously that sooner or later this woman and I might taste each other's candies and fruits, and brighten up this gulag of a place. It wasn't conceit, it was the underground river of my yearning, which would inspire a superhuman effort to find my way to her and was now beginning to erode my resolve to remain chaste and whole. I was at the onset of a swoon. I knew the signs: I see her in my little apartment, lit just so, diminutive in my big chair, as I read to her, as I fuss with things to make her comfortable. When I'm on the street I want to stop strangers and tell them that I have wonderful news.

"I'm sorry? What does that mean in English?" I asked, wide-eyed. The men whirled around as one beast with many heads to stare at me. My question apparently suggested to them that I had crossed over, that I was the point man for their dreams about her. I would be their threshold guardian, their Sherpa.

"I was down and out in Berlin," she translated, and sighed again, a wind that seemed to shake the room.

"And therefore what?"

"*Und also nichts*," she said, "And therefore nothing. Forget it."

And therefore nothing*ness* I think she is saying, which I

extrapolated through a series of syllogistic steps to signify a special interest in the libido, because I have a theory that no one is more evolved libidinally or puts out with more vigor than a death-obsessed nihilist. If the sentiments of our diplomate in human sexuality and our Freudians are correct, she suffers from a neurotic fixation that can only find resolution by making *me*, the only associate that has resisted her, the object of transference; only the unattainable Other can bring her to the death-orgasm she seeks. On the other hand, according to our Eastern Studies man, in mythological terms she might be Durga the Unattainable; and I, Siddhartha, in resisting her blandishments, attempt to purify my consciousness and live in the last *chakra*, the one above the head, altogether outside the degraded husk of the body and its omnivorous thirsts and disappointments. Our neuroscience team, amused by what they regarded as the poetry of my questions, suggested I read their paper, "The Chemistry of Eros," and especially to have a look at the instinctive behavioral responses to the effusion of serotonin and oxytocin. *"You're in rut, mister!"* they shouted, and giggled in unison.

Later that day in the cafeteria I saw her sitting alone. I stopped in mid-stride. I almost ran away but I did some fast deep breathing and walked toward her. As I got closer I recited *don't do this, don't do this, don't do this* in cadence with my steps.

"May I join you?" I asked, looking beyond her, as if I might choose another table. She waved a hand in a dramatic gesture that said: *Fate will cause you to crash into me in this turn of the wheel, or it won't.* The orbiting associates turned as one body.

"So. What's your area?" she asked after I sat.

"The Talmud. But *secular*," I said, emphatically, not wanting her to think of me as rabbinical or neutered.

"Oh, you're a Jew?" she asked.

"Yes. Ashkenazi. Belarus."

"*Really.* Well, I'm a philosemite. When I was a little girl, I had fantasies of being a famous Jewess with a salon for artistes and literati. I love the Jewish people. I love all things Jewish."

She seemed insane and ridiculous, but my desire deepened, undiluted by the thought, supporting the zoological reading offered up by the neuroscience team. I tried to be languid, to appear as though I was only peripherally aware of her because my brain was fulminating.

"Hm? Really? Well, that's uncomfortable."

"Oh? Uncomfortable? How so? Make your case."

I appeared thoughtful. Every day in the seminar rooms I am observed for the quality of my thoughtfulness. I'm good at it, and I've used it without shame. I study the posture in my wardrobe mirror and I'm very secure in what I see there. Very smart, very together, an important intellect ruminating. *Idiot,* I counseled myself, reeling out of control.

"Well," I began, "*dicto simpliciter*, the sweeping generalization. The bad Jews are swept in with the good. This subsumes a diverse population of idiosyncratic individuals into a single treatment—in your case, loving them. And of course that's good. But then if things don't go well, such as if a Jew shortchanges you a nickel, or eats with his mouth open, ruining your lunch, you hate them all instead of love them all, because to you they are still indistinguishable. So now they are all vermin, and you must kill them. If you want to frighten a Jew, tell him you love all of his people."

I was so tense I had delivered my speech in one breath and ended with a wheezy squeak. I had been so fixated on the labial, cherry-bud lips and the fluorescent milky face that I wasn't sure what I'd said.

She studied me.

"Alright, I'm wrong," she said.

"What?"

"I'm wrong. If you want to gloat, knock yourself out. I find it exciting to be dominated intellectually."

"You do?" I gaped at her, eyes wide, my carefully constructed persona wrecked.

"Yes. I'm always right, so being wrong is an adventure. Look at you, you smart man. Take your reward. Enjoy your moment."

She wins a moral victory by capitulation. She implies that intellectually she exists in an elevated, rarified realm, above my childish and petty desire to be right. She'd infantilized me but then anointed me—a clever, contradictory, paralyzing maneuver. In her perspective, therefore, I'm a baby with a big brain. My only options now were to prove to her that I was indeed not a baby, or to imagine that she was attracted only to man-babies—and then to be the very best one at the Institute.

Later that day, jumpy and fixated, at last lost to her, I entered her seminar room while she was showing a newsreel about the collapse of the Weimar Republic. Wagner trumpeted the Gotterdammerung scratchily on the sound track. She sat in the middle of the room; her brilliant, suited rear blossomed through the opening at the back of the chair, each lobe a planet. Her shoes were off under the desk, baring perfect little ivory feet. I gasped.

There are events in life whose advent can be mapped in retrospect; I had been on a path without knowing it, and I knew now that every red light, every nap, wrong turn, distraction, hesitation, accident, chore, every blink of the eyes were all in fact calculated corrections on a path of Stoic inevitability to this woman and her riddles. She came rushing up at me like the ground to a man who has jumped off a building. My studies offered no direction or solace; the Talmud addresses only familial love, God-love, and the impurity of menstruating women. My studies are already an infinite emergency, a perpetual crisis of meaning, and now this.

I hesitated for a moment, then pitched myself into the abyss. I stalked up to her formally, as if I had pressing business that would explain my bursting into her seminar. I came very close; the associates gaped before I'd even reached her, having witnessed our meeting in the cafeteria. I leaned down to her. Startled, she tried to pull away, but I stayed with her as she moved. I pressed my face close to her ear, as if to whisper an important message, just barely within the limits of propriety.

My face now nearly buried in the crook of her neck, I wasn't prepared for the smell of her. I sniffed her, two deep, windy sniffs, and grew lightheaded. I faltered.

"I was wrong about your comment about Jews," I whispered, my lips brushing her ear. "I made assumptions about you. A tu quoque fallacy. I was foolish. Unfair. Even rude. I'm so sorry. You were right and I was wrong."

I drew back a little to see her face; she sat rigidly, staring at the screen. Her breath came in small gasps. It looked like submission to me, so at last I threw myself at her without caution and breathed hot love in her ear: "Oh, my god. My lovely genius. My honey pot. My perfect perfectness," and then, bent over with my back to the associates, I whispered a long exegesis of love and obsession as images of Germans rioting in the streets of the Weimar Republic were projected on us from behind.

Ach! Mein Gott! Unglaublich! Ja! Ja! she cried out that night, in the back seat of my car in the deserted parking lot. *Oh! My God! Unbelievable! Yes! Yes!*

Six

THE THEATER OF SERVITUDE

"A man unto myself," I like to say, to relate to whoever might be interested that I'm not lonesome, but determined to be alone. I wasn't always this way. I used to be a very social man, but I think now is the right time in world history, in this billowing of the plasma pool, to be alone. I have no friends. I have no women, very few things, no witnesses. Now everyone and everything is subsumed into a deep commiseration with myself. I'm the president and the people of the Sovereign Nation of Myself.

Months ago, in what seems to be another life, a man I

knew told me his mother had died. He cried and shook. His nose ran. He said he'd loved his mother and that he couldn't imagine the world without her in it. I sat there with my head hanging to avoid eye contact, mining myself for a scrap of grief, yet found nothing but the distress of being watched for the performance of my sorrow. Finally I leapt up, pulled him into my arms, and put my cheek on his so he couldn't see the grin that could never be explained.

Sometime along the way I had lost the spunk to take part in the gore of relationships; I could feel only astonishment.

Now I appear to have rescued myself from the obligatory rites of struggle with other men. Of women I continue to know nothing. I speak as little as I can. "This," I say to a man behind a counter, pointing. I live in my bed as much as I can. I don't understand a great deal else but I understand the qualities and meaning of my bed. I think of it as the capital of my sovereign nation. I only crawl out of it to go to work, and I climb right back in when I get home.

I work in the lobby of a residence hotel. I humiliate myself daily, but for a purpose: I study servitude, and I'm good at it. It's right for me to serve now; I was never very good at making sense of how to conduct myself, and to serve is to practice someone else's righteous and exact plan for relations. It's time for me to submit—that's my choice at this moment, my art, and I embrace it.

My small cubicle is in the dead center of the immense, blinding-white modernistic lobby. It's the right station for a man that prefers to be diminished; I think of the lobby as my Theater of Servitude. In my cubicle I can be seen from anywhere in the giant space, a little nucleus at work for the happiness and welfare of the residents, who tell me regularly that my small spectacle reassures them, like a statue of a local hero in a town square.

I ask to be called Bobby, the diminutive inevitably applied to a grown man who serves. I make sure to keep my shiny, almost blue-black hair combed neatly. I wear a beautifully tailored tunic, ultramarine blue with narrow red piping. I think it makes me look very handsome, almost electric against the blinding white of the lobby, which might seem to be a conceit that contradicts my agenda of humility; but I can think of it as a little bonus of service to the residents, who I believe would rather be served by a handsome man than a homely one, a little libidinous moment in the middle of their gruesome workday. Who wouldn't want that?

At night in my apartment, in my full-length mirror, I study the movements associated with servitude, and I've become a kind of expert. I went to the library to do research on butlering, specifically the art of European Continental service; how, for example, to appear to be a man's subordinate with a few minimal gestures and postures and yet somehow appear to be his equal in the larger notion of things. How to be omnipresent and invisible at once. How to scold a man with a cold look if he tries to carry his own bags, how the look might suggest that if he does his own work he might be a pretender from the working classes. The servant, not the master, is the architect of his servitude.

I make the most timid client feel that being served is his natural right, that God loves him. Every man gets a shot, every citizen gets his own flunky. The more timid they are, the more profound my attention; this is my discipline. I've learned to make him think *Oh, here is someone who can see that I'm a man of quality.* I never put my hands above my head. I keep my heels together. Making my hands into a little steeple comes naturally to me. I appear to have no opinions; if I'm asked to give one about, for example, a political issue, I say, my eyes down, "I'm afraid I wouldn't know about that, sir." I certainly *do* know about that, sir, but let's suspend disbelief for a moment and make you feel like somebody special, an effort that I throw my whole heart and talent into with absolute sincerity.

Occasionally, though, I hate the man I'm serving; a presumptuous man, a swaggering man who seems to move through a trumped-up world of his own making; and if I can't help loathing him, I keep it to myself. I think about slapping his face and I grind my teeth. *Good morning, Mr. Fuckface,* I think, while giving him my most deferent nod and most handsome smile. *Evening, sir, I hope you die soon.*

I had been interviewed by the entire management team, a species of suited men at whom all I can do is gape. The head man, a very old man, said they were looking for a people person, did I think I was one? Do you like people? People are essentially good, don't you think? What do you think? I stared at him, while in my peripheral vision I saw the others lean in as a unit to hear my answer. Oh, yes, I am, I said, I *am* a people person, I think that people are essentially good, I said, and that if they are treated as such, it will bring out the best in them. Of course I think nothing of the kind. "Life is a God-damned, stinking, treacherous game and nine hundred and ninety-nine men out of a thousand are bastards," a luminary once said, a sentiment I enthusiastically share.

They told me that an important part of my job would be to greet the tenants and visitors as they come in the door from the street. Be clean and look friendly and welcoming, they said, this is the job. You're a good-looking man, they said, you'll be the first thing they'll see, and they'll think, what a good-looking man, this must be a place for good-looking people, therefore I'm good-looking too—and then they'll be happy. This is a very important position, they said, to make people happy. As important as the president, they said, because a good operation depends on the performance of even the least of men. And stand up straight, they said, there's no slouching in business.

I was given basic tools by the managers that connect me only minimally to the clientele: a telephone, a pencil and pad, a list, a pocket comb, and a piece of cloth to buff my shoes. When they gave me the little kit with my supplies I stared down at them, thinking of the pitiful objects as the totems of my disgrace; but later I thought of them as simple and eloquent—all any man should need to get along.

Nevertheless the telephone is a source of anxiety. I was told by the management team that I should try to be kind on the telephone. Try to be kind, they said, life is hard, always assume that whoever calls can use a little kindness in the middle of a typically gruesome day in this goddamn shit-hole city. So be kind on the telephone, they said in a kindly way, meaning it.

This is a conundrum to me, because except for my rehearsed gestures of servitude I wouldn't know the first thing to say to someone who needed kindness. I'm a motherless monkey, hugging myself, consoling only to myself, and if there's a revolution or a natural catastrophe or an apocalypse on the horizon, everyone else had better find it in themselves to expect nothing from me. If I wanted to be kind, I would remind every caller that something just terrible is likely to happen to them in the future, and probably soon, so they'd better get ready. *What are you thinking,* I'd shout into the phone, *that there WON'T be a catastrophe? That everything is okay? Have you read the newspapers?! Have you looked out of your window?! Go look right now,* I'd counsel, *and then we'll see if you can think of a good reason to take another goddamn breath!*

And, in the service of kindness, I might advise that they live as though it were their last day, although personally I think I would spend that day thrashing in grief, shrieking and tearing my clothes.

So I'm not good at the telephone. When it rings, I jump out of my skin:

"Hello? Yes?"

"Hello. I was wondering . . ."

"Yes?" I say it louder.

"I was wondering if you have any apartments?"

"Yes?" I'm shouting now.

"Yes? Are you saying yes? Yes, you do?"

"Do what, sir?" Still shouting.

"I'm sorry, you said *yes,* didn't you? To my question?" He speaks in a normal voice, as though a man isn't shouting at him.

I paused. Why did the man say he was sorry? Christ, I don't want his sorrow. I don't want anyone else's sorrow, I'm consumed by my own, and I have nothing useful or relevant to say about it. It seems rude to bring your sorrow to someone else, who you can assume certainly has enough of it on his own plate, given the state of things in the world, which would take about a millisecond to figure out if one had any social instincts at all. Here a perfect stranger finds me and within a heartbeat he tells me about his sorrow.

"Hello?"

"Oh. Yes, sir, I did say yes, I mean, yes, I understand your question, sir."

"You do?" This man seems insane to me, without affect. Or drugged. Or a lovely, gentle man.

"Yes, sir."

"And?"

"And what, sir?"

"And do you have apartments?"

I'd like to shake this man. Does he have a spine? I would have wanted to shoot me by now. "Do you mean *me*, sir? Do *I* have apartments?"

"Yes."

I paused again, startled by his question.

"Why, yes, I do have an apartment, sir. Of course I have an apartment."

"May I see it?"

"You'd like to see my apartment?"

"Yes."

Why does this man without affect want to see my apartment? I don't understand most of what is said to me. Everyone seems insane to me.

"I suppose, sir."

"I'm sorry? You suppose what?"

"I'm just supposing."

"Who *is* this?"

"Excuse me, sir, but are you pointing at someone? How could I know who it is? I can't see through the telephone."

"I mean, who am I *speaking* to?"

Ah. This is the big question, the one I have been studying since I was a small boy always on the verge of tears; I stopped to think about it for a minute, to give the man my latest and best speculation about exactly to whom he might be speaking. But hearing nothing, he soon hung up.

If he'd been patient and given me a few minutes to think

about his question on that day, I would have told him this:

Three syllogisms constitute an organizing principle:

1. I move from Point A to Point B, tiring myself, and find that the conditions at Point B are never different from those at Point A: Therefore why move?

2. Everything told to me is incomprehensible, consequently I can reasonably conclude that everything *I* say is incomprehensible: Therefore why speak?

3. Every thought I have is trapped in subjectivity and consequently can't be agreed upon as truth: Therefore why think?

And I would have told him this: Poor all of us.

Journal entry
*December 18, 20_*

A scientist has proposed the construction of an immense mechanical clock, on the scale of a city block, where it can be seen every day by every citizen. It ticks once a year, tolls once a century, and a cuckoo emerges once every thousand years. It is conceived as a contemplative object that will evoke thoughts about causality; we will see it and think, in some form, that everything we do will radiate forward, forever.

A small video camera trained on the front entrance tells me if there is someone entering the lobby whom I'm expected to attend to. I watch the monitor all day long for its elementary drama; no one comes in, then someone comes in. I find it very reassuring; someone always comes in, I always know the end of the story.

At my interview the management company seemed to imply that for my small salary I was expected to pitch myself into fistfights with criminals who I will see entering the lobby on my monitor. But I plan to hide when they come, hoping their interest in trouble will have been satisfied by Mr. A and Mr. M, the two tiny, ancient, and ghostly men who are always in the big stuffed chairs in the lobby. I'm sure they'll die of natural causes in those chairs—and soon—and I'm always anxious about it. Mr. M, the more inert of the two, always seems from our distance to have already died; when I get concerned I cross the lobby to him, get very close, and look to see if the large vein in his forehead is still pulsing. I walk slowly, as if I'm walking underwater, wincing, not wanting to know. I always hope I'll be suddenly called away. Or I'll be fired suddenly. Or that there'll be a cataclysm, like a meteor strike, so catastrophic it will render his death insignificant. Anything, so that I don't have to attend to his death. I can't face that my acts of sympathy will be witnessed, and I know I'll start to laugh, absolutely, not because I won't be heartbroken at the death of a good old man, but because, as I've said, I've lost my understanding of relations, and astonishment is about all I feel anymore.

I read that a dying man will shit himself, and if that happens I will just run right out the front door into the street, throwing my tunic, pad, pencil, list, pocket comb, and shoe buffing cloth over my shoulder as I run.

I wait until late at night when they've fallen asleep in the stuffed chairs, and then I carry their papery bodies back to their room one by one and put them in their twin beds like children, my head craned away from their vapors. Then I wander around the room, examining their few objects; a small globe whose text is in a script I don't recognize, a worn book of homilies, a cheaply framed picture of a small boy cut from a newspaper, one that fades a degree more each time I see it; I'm not much for ephemera, I like hard ground, but I have wondered if the disappearance of the image will coincide with the passing of the old men.

They're always in their stuffed chairs, like memento mori, like threshold guardians.

Journal entry
October 2, 20___

The philosopher Wittgenstein, when he met others socially, was very conscious of his temptation to be dishonest, to make a good impression by appearing to be more and better than he was, to perform received social conventions. His response to these rules was to break all of them. At least one formidable personality said about this behavior that she always thought of him with "awe and alarm."

Several times in his life he made arrangements to make a formal confession to a friend or acquaintance. Wittgenstein asked that the confessor sit across from him and listen to a complete recitation of his bad behavior, including the confession that he had tried to appear less Jewish than he was. No one wanted to do it; they were always uncomfortable, but Wittgenstein insisted.

His lectures, each a new and thorough philosophical work, were given without notes or preparation; declarations would be followed by long silences during which his face was intensely alive and his hands moved expressively, as if he were still speaking.

It appeared to others that Wittgenstein was suffocating in the deep structure of things; that each breath he took and each word he used was an event to examine philosophically. It was believed by everyone that he suffered mightily; he claimed the wish to die from a very early age. Three of his four brothers committed suicide. When he was told that he would die from his cancer, he replied, "Good." On his deathbed he told his last visitors, "Tell them I've had a wonderful life."

I've read 5,000 books in my life. I have an eidetic memory; I can sit with my eyes closed and turn every page and see with absolutely clarity every word I've ever consumed. This fact changes nothing about my social being, no one cares about how well read I am, and it has no real application. I confess to a secret pleasure at the irony of my groveling to serve the residents, when I bend over for them to pick up their things with my ass in the air. They'll never get the joke, though; on their deathbeds they'll think about a life that was lived just as life should be; they were disciplined and clean, they worked hard and got their share, and it doesn't matter at all that they never got around to reading books. But then, what were they supposed to do? Be like me? I look into their faces again, more deeply this time, and think: I want to feel like they do, just let me sink into this life like a baby into its bathwater. If only I could!

When I was a boy, already having read five hundred books or so, an older man in the neighborhood demanded that I prove I was real. I had seen the man passing by before; this time he suddenly veered off the sidewalk to me as I sat on the stoop of my building and appeared to take it upon himself to give me a philosophical lesson. Without explaining, he insisted that I demonstrate I was actually present. I felt immediately anxious; in a high, agitated voice I insisted that of course I was *absolutely* present, and *absolutely* real, that the man could see me and hear me, and that was all the proof anyone should need. The man slowly turned his back on me and, even more slowly, with a theatrical flourish he put his fingers in his ears, elbows up, to illustrate that I no longer existed in his senses and perhaps not even in his memory. I knew at that moment that it was no contest; a grown man had set a linguistic trap for a callow boy.

The new idea that one's sense of being was so fragile struck me hard. Who asked the question? Who gave the answer? If the man was right, and I actually didn't exist, what was I supposed to do? Drop dead? Look up girls' dresses? I got very frightened and began to cry; I sobbed, rubbing my fists in my eyes, while the man remained with his back to me, posturing, his fingers still in his ears, blind and deaf to a young boy's existential crisis. At last he walked off, very slowly and dramatically, not looking back. His fingers were still in his ears, elbows up, as he passed out of sight. Although he lived close by, the man never looked at or spoke to me again, leaving me to grudgingly admire his rigor as a mentor.

That night in bed I decided that things were at best ephemeral, and that perhaps even a simple declarative sentence was an enigma, a shadow of metaphysical truth. (I was a very smart little kid. I had a little library in my room, and its flagship text was *Basic Philosophy for Preteens*. "*Cogito, ergo cogito, cogito*," I postulated, laying in bed, "I think, therefore I think, I think," and woke up the next morning feeling like a holy boy, who had, by virtue of my traumatic lesson with the man, begun to look into the deep structure of things.)

Now a grown man and still disposed to this kind of

thinking, I enter any room edgy and alert, with the attention I might give a fistfight. I believe that any thoughtful person might think about the risk of crossing any threshold. As I move through a room, I can see fast glances, transgression moldering in them, just under a thin skin of civility. That human beings are autonomous is an atrocious plan to me, an absolute emergency, and if faith is necessary for the human embrace, I don't have any left. The immense gulf between two beings is filled with bad news. Everyone appears as a vulgar corruption of *me*; the simple difference in the shape of a face, or the hint of a bone protruding to the surface, like me, but not me. Men live and die eluding me. A man looks into a mirror; where am *I* in it?

Everything I've learned amounts to this: we bump into one another, bang into a trade, crash into the grave.

Journal entry
December 2, 20___

In the 1960s, the New York Museum of Natural History invited a New Guinea mud-man to visit Manhattan. He was given a room at the 92nd Street Y, and generally moved about the city on his own. Although concessions were made to modesty, he wore his mud-suit in the streets; mud was, after all, his formal dress. He said that he wanted most to visit places of work; it was there, he said, that he would understand most about our culture. He was given many gifts to take back with him to New Guinea, but after he was gone it was discovered that he had abandoned all the gifts in his room.

I live in Apartment 100; I get it free with the job. I seem to have made the apartment into a kind of incubator, a skin constructed only for my pleasure and the proportions of my body. I no longer regard my rooms as separate from me, as though the space between my body and what I've made is saturated with my affection for it. It's the nest of a solitary man. Like Zeus, who swallowed his wife and gave birth to the full-grown Athena through his head, my rooms bloom from me. Grandiose, but who gives a damn, who's looking? I'm both the sovereign and the people in one.

All of my furniture is arranged for my extreme comfort. I live in absolute silence. I've laid thick carpets on the floors; that and a maze of shelves suppress whatever sounds I make as I move through my rooms. All I can hear are my own breath and my blood roaring through my veins. The telephone is only a concession to necessity; I don't make friendly calls. It rings rarely, and when it does, as I've said, I jump out of my skin.

Once in a while someone knocks on my door; I stop what I'm doing, and I don't move or breathe until I'm sure they're gone. I have a habit of seeing things simultaneously from an elevated view: I can see the top of the head of the stranger (it can only be a stranger, there are only strangers) outside the door, and myself inside, in mid-stride, holding my breath and trembling, trying to be still. At one time I wondered who they might have been; in my mind I followed them through the city, through the day, to their beds. I don't think about them anymore.

I've cut a hole in my curtain, and I sit and look through the hole to the street; this is the sum of my social life, and even this is waning. I don't like to leave my apartment; when I have to I always want to hole up and try again the next day to face the circumspect way I've come to move through the streets.

I have a single bed in a tiny alcove off the kitchen. Every morning is the same; up early and apprehensive from a rough, electric sleep. When I look in my mirror I always hope to see something vivid; instead I see the stricken look, as if I'm looking out of my window and watching the approach of someone shouting bad news. The folds in my face hold a grievance, my posture seems to tell the story of a blow.

No one comes here. Where would they sit? If they break down the door and find me dead, they'll conclude that I was insane. Presumably, unless there is some dramatic change in my life, this is exactly what will happen.

Journal entry
*August 2, 20_*

Names of Deities:

brahma allah vishnu siva krishna juggernaut buddha ra baal thor odin mumbo-jumbo jesus yahweh ishtar kali kwan yin wakantanka quetzlqoatl itsa-ma conticsi-viracocha kumush kukulkan good genius tutelary genius jupiter demiurge familiar spirit sybil fairy fay sylphid ariel peri nymph nereid oread sea-maid banshee benshee ormuz oberon titiana hamadryad naiad mermaid kelpie ondine nixie

There is something to living alone; who knows what people do when there aren't any witnesses, when you're in the mind of no one? I can sleep in odd positions, rant, play-act scenes of unspeakable violence or romantic love. I can dress up, I can be stupid and melodramatic; who's to know?

I wonder what it might be like to be a twin, or a triplet—a three-bodied Narcissus swimming only with my selves in a perfumed amniotic bliss, where everything is me, a honeymoon of thought thinking itself.

Halfway down my long hallway, on the other side of the thin apartment wall is the bedroom of the man next door, in apartment 102; I've calculated that his sleeping head is inches away from me as I make the passage, the wall a thin membrane between me and his peculiarities, his obscene privacies. I'm certain I can hear him breathing. I was horrified by this discovery. When I have to go down the hall, I move as quickly as I can past the sleeping head, repressing the urge to punch the wall as hard as I can where I think the head is. Hugging the opposite wall and sliding past, I imagine an elevated view, thinking of his alien head on an alien floral pattern, dreaming a dream without me in it.

When I see him in the building it's all I can do to keep from running down the hall away from him, shouting at him to get away.

In the middle of the apartment, lit by a tiny circle of light, is a small framed antique print of the plant *Atropa belladonna*. I put it where I can see it from virtually everywhere in the apartment. It has a winged stalk, and the berries are held in the palm of the star-shaped calyx as though they're being offered. Its Latinate name is from the Greek Atropa, one of the Fates, who cuts the thread of life irreparably. The berries are impenetrable, inky-black snake eyes with a nucleus of light like a diamond pupil. When eaten, they cause deep blushing, hallucinations, fits of frenzy and crying out, and at last an eruption of language that I would deliver from my window, startling the people in the street.

Then paralysis, coma, and death. I know that paralysis will come at the last moment, in the most theatrical posture of oratory; and that's how I'll be found, as if I'm already a statue.

I'm not suicidal; the berries are a memento mori. I look up and see them, and think, oh, right, *death*, and I'm ready for some fast pleasure. I don't understand why we were made to know that our death is imminent. What kind of plan is that? *Be here now, man*, I say out loud to myself.

I can turn any time of the day or night, from reading, from sleep, and see the berries calling to me, *Here we are, whenever you're ready; deliver your soliloquy.*

Nevertheless, in the absence of anything that might be called an authentic life, I have my collections.

I've made my apartment into a Byzantine maze of shelves, from floor to ceiling, an oasis of stories, notebooks, scraps, notes on napkins, exotica. I use all of my money and resources to gather the material. I read everything that drifts my way. From my cubicle in the lobby I've come to be able to read the mannerisms of a small group that suggest a good story is being told: the animation of the story-teller, and his audience so engaged that they forget their own vanities and gape at him. I wander over to them pretending to do a chore and listen secretly. I remember, in perfect detail, the timing, the nuances, the text of the story.

Each entry is recorded carefully in my oversized ledger made of handmade papers, bound in bird's-eye maple veneer covers and wrapped with thick seaman's rope, a beautiful object that I made myself. One dated entry in my careful hand appears on each page. It sits on a small, sturdy table I found in the street on the day discarded furniture is picked up by the city. My old, oversized stuffed chair, which I chose for its pattern of utopian World's Fair monuments, sits beside it in the little shrine-like corner.

I can't say what qualities make something that I've read or heard have significance. I imagine all the things and events and thoughts and histories in the world as a miasma—fulminating, cooking, incomprehensible. Once in a long while a little light escapes and delivers something that makes sense in a way I can't explain. I know it when I see it.

My knowledge is encyclopedic, but finally I can't make sense of things. A theory of everything, of how things work—which I long for—escapes me; but I rush to its evidence like a pup to its mother.

On the single wall without shelves, miniaturized and framed, are the illustrated cosmologies of 147 organizing systems. The Hippocratic Oath is there, as are the Code of Hammurabi; the proportions of the Golden Mean; the list of the classical Logical Fallacies; Roget's Synopsis of Categories; the Periodic Tables; the Diamond Sutra of Buddha, *Robert's Rules of Order*; the Pentatonic Scale; the Constitution of the Iroquois Nation; a fragment of Sophocles' *Oedipus Rex*, the fifteenth-century dramatization of the Easter Trope; a treatise on architecture by Vitruvius; a still from the first moving picture, the Lumière brothers' arrival of a train at a station; and all the known alphabets of the world: Etruscan, Piceni, Venetic, Italic, Alpine, Runic, Sumerian cuneiform, Akkadian cuneiform, Egyptian, Proto-Elamite, Proto-Indic, Cretan, Hittite, Eblaite, Hattic, Hurrian, Luwian, Palaic, Ugarit, Cherokee, Chinese, Japanese, Korean, North Semitic, Canaanite, Aramaic, Square Hebrew, Brahmi, Kharosthi, Siddha, Devanagari, Sanskrit, Sabean, Greek, Cyrillic, Etruscan, Arabic, Kufic, Nashki, Latin, International Phonetic.

The tiny wall seems vast to me. I know I'm in there somewhere; some constellation can be plotted that has my form.

❧

Journal entry
March 18, 20_____

Names of belief systems:
adventist   arianist   puseyist   atheist   animist   pantheist
shark-worshipper   ethicist   polytheist   materialist   monist   pos-
itivist   heathen   papist   theist   deist   agnostic   rabbist   sufi
maw-worm   wowser   fire-worshipper   zoroastrian   rastafarian
dunker   glassite   mormon   supra-lapsarian   ecologist   hagiog-
rapher   shintoist   secular humanist   hedonist   libertine   sybarite
devil-worshipper   ascetic   sabbatarian   vegan   utopian   hutterite
altruist

Journal entry
October 21, 20_____

"Cynicism" of ancient Greece and Rome derives its name from the Greek word for "Dog." The loose aggregate of cynics, never a formal school of philosophy, rejected refined philosophy, believing that a simple man could know all there is to know.

The objective of Cynicism was self-sufficiency, autarkeia, and any quality through which freedom was attained was regarded as a virtue: callousness, apathy, ruggedness, endurance, theft. The "lower" animals were emulated for their disinterest in clothing, shelter, and the artificial preparation of food. The cynic disregarded law, convention, public opinion, reputation, honor, and dishonor.

Aristotle refers to the fourth-century cynic Diogenes of Sinope as "The Dog," an epithet Diogenes seems to have embraced. At feasts the guests threw bones to him as they would a dog. He pissed on the bones. He often shit publicly to end his discourses. He was known to masturbate and perform other sexual acts in public.

Diogenes did little philosophizing other than to imply that doing so was a waste of time. He sought to live a public and exemplary life of autonomy; he lived on the street in a tub, in full view of the public.

He was said to have asked for a handout from a bad-tempered man who said, "Yes, if you can persuade me." "If I had the power to persuade you," said Diogenes, "I would persuade you to hang yourself."

On a voyage to Aegina he was captured by pirates, conveyed to Crete, and put up for sale as a slave. When he was asked what he could do he replied, "Govern men." He told the man to give notice, in case anybody wanted to purchase a master for himself.

At another time Diogenes was sunning himself when Alexander the Great stood over him and said, "Ask of me anything you like." He replied, "Get out of my light."

Diogenes probably died at Corinth, at the age of ninety. A marble column, topped by the figure of a dog, was raised over his tomb.

I'm in love with the woman in apartment 204.

She isn't beautiful or pretty—but lovely, specifically. I studied her face for weeks. I thought I identified a trace of damage, something that illuminated her alarmingly pale face. Of course this was the deathblow to my determination to resist falling in love with her; evidence of the flaw that would make her anticipate and embrace flaws in the world, in me.

Like a man in trouble who burns to be safe at home again, all of my thoughts soon led to the woman.

My emotional life has no place on the job, so to love her is an endless negotiation, through subtle moves and coded language. For a short time the apartment next to hers was empty; I let myself in and leaned on the wall to be close to her, to hear her moving.

I saw her with a man once; he had entered and walked across the lobby to ask me what her apartment number was. He was a handsome, self-possessed man; I had the impulse to slap his face. He'd startled me with his question; I stared at him and then I told him no one of that name lived here, but he insisted he had the right address and I had to confess and deliver her to him. All that night I was in agony imagining him naked and in lurid positions with the woman I love, which is to say, regarding these issues, that he wins, that all men will regard him therefore as the owner of *me*. And then for days I compulsively imagined them being intimate, which brought on short bouts of stinging tears, repressed brutally by me. Once in my cubicle I was so struck by a thought regarding them that I burst into sobs, three rhythmic, deep heaves. An echo in the vast lobby made it sound like a sob sobbed for the whole world. *That ... will ... not ... happen ... again.*

Journal entry
December 6, 20_____

Names of Devils:

ahrimanes satan lucifer belial sammael beelzebub author of evil old serpent prince of this world the foul fiend prince of the power of the air angel of the bottomless pit mammon friar rush inhabitant of pandemonium the cloven foot the worm that never dies cacodemon incubus succubus titan shedim moloch fury harpy ef-freet djinn deev lamia bo-gie bo-gle nis kobold flibbertigibbet brownie puck bad fairy robin goodfellow dwerger oaf changeling nix pigwidgeon will-o'-the-wisp erl king boggart lemures necks loup-garou

I believe I am truly in love. I regard myself as *having* the woman. I'm a minor functionary on the periphery of her life, and chances are good she has no thoughts about me whatsoever. Still, I regard myself as "having" the woman, in the sense that from the moment I decided I love her she has lived vividly and hotly in my mind, and isn't that the best that can be between a man and a woman anyway? When someone we love dies, we like to think about them continuing to live in our hearts and minds; but I believe that another being, living or otherwise, can only manifest themselves in one's heart and mind in *any* event, so it makes good sense to me to construct my love for this woman as a kind of willful hallucination, exactly to my needs, without the rigorous business of an actual relationship in the flesh, in real time, and without the inevitable waning of exuberance about the good luck to have found the perfect love.

My association with this woman *is* perfect, by virtue of the lack of neurotic projections, different favorite colors, sleeping arrangements, food, a constellation of irreconcilable difference. I know about myself that I can be sulky sometimes, and I see no reason why a woman, especially one that I love, should have to tolerate this aspect of my character. And I'm not naïve. I'm certain that the woman also has undesirable traits of some kind; in real life, what if she's ignorant, or ridiculous, or hoards food, or screams in her sleep? What if she can't read? I invent her, but I give her fine qualities. Absent from this relationship is the sad and shabby moment when, in time, I'd have to reckon with the guilty injustice of glaring at her because she has a little piece of food stuck on her lip. And the suspicion that she will always be other, alien, impenetrable, not *me*, that her inner organs, her spit, her tastes, the shape of her ears, ghastly and incomprehensible.

I *do* have a woman, I think with contentment, even understanding that she is likely only a repository for my conceit. I tell no one about this, certain that they would regard me as peculiar, or even dangerous.

Weeks passed before I could even bring to full consciousness my obsession with the woman. It wasn't sexual. It was much later that I even acknowledged the fact of her sex, and then it was with a distress I couldn't name. The looming image of her naked body brought on vertigo. I didn't want it, I wanted to concentrate on other aspects of her, and I shook the thought out of my head.

I'm convinced that the woman has a good story to tell of, say, some extreme of human life or proportion, something that would account for her special presence. I'm certain she suffers the ironic isolation of one like her; as a repository, a nucleus of meaning, she is a Beautiful Lamb denied the relief of an unremarkable existence. Whatever I might imagine as the person seems inaccessible, imprisoned in the lovely, milky body.

I confess to myself the selfishness of my interest in her; and that I construct her to suit my desire. I want only to sink into that pool. In my story about her she receives with good faith the unlovely account of me, a hollow man, a man with no gifts, no advice, nothing to offer but the inert tale of an approximate life. Other men have their ways of being in love, I have mine.

I write feverish love letters to her. I don't send them; I keep them in my book:

Dear____,

I love you. I don't know anything about you, your real qualities, your history. As flesh, you're inconceivable to me. You're a shade; but you billow like a flame outside of me. I'm exhausted by my brief sightings of you, only a small moment in your aloof and lonesome trajectory, far away and as silent and melancholy as a satellite. I'm moving in my own arc, looking through my telescope at you right now, trying to determine if there's life there, if it's like me.

The life that I invent for us is full and fervent. Often in my fantasies about you I explain to you at length my position on subjects in the newspaper; I stand and make a speech and posture dramatically, while you sit in our big stuffed chair and listen quietly to me. You don't speak. You never speak. It suits you not to speak; things are just as they should be; why talk about it?

Once, in my daydreams, you found and punished someone who had hurt me, humiliated them cleverly, and then slapped them to the ground. Once when I acted stupidly, you took me by the collar, lifted me off my feet, and shook me ruthlessly, to make the point. And there was a poignant, lazy event in which you lay inert, in a cozy stupor, while I inspected your body thoroughly, top to bottom, until I was drowsy with pleasure, and then I slept without dreaming. I didn't linger on the vagina; I was thinking about other implications, other meanings of you.

If I tell you what I wear, how I sleep, what I eat, what I read, the things I dream about; my tics, antagonisms, affectations, enthusiasms, and afflictions; what aches; how I grieve, sin, languish, collapse; what I own, who knows me, the stories I tell again and again; the set of my face, my posture, how I greet and say goodbye, my scars, measurements, stride, records, all the elements of the idea of me, all the mean mundane forensic evidence of me—wouldn't this be enough? Do you need any more? What passes between two people in the same room but trouble, after all? I invent you out of the few salient clues I have. My invention is my lover, my friend, my work. I draw the idea of you over me like a blanket.

You're perfect; what I have to give you is a perfect idea of you; sublime, vivid, deathless, beautiful. My Beautiful Lamb. And I love you so much.

Sincerely,

———————————

Wednesday nights off. Mosh pit night, at the last punk club in the city. This is where I remember the world I once lived in amicably, where I pitch myself into it, the event I keep for myself to commune, touch other beings, smell them. You could say this is where I love fully. I'm always excited when I stand at my mirror, suit up, and gel my blue-black hair into something repugnant.

All middle-aged men, the real thing, no crybabies. Furious pogoing, an absolute Götterdämmerung. There is a certain lovely harmony in smashing a man in the face with his full consent.

Later, when I'm lying in my bed thinking in retrospect about the satisfactions of the evening, I feel as if I'd really shared an intimacy with someone. I'm in the swim at last, I've entered the slipstream; then a sweet sleep, then back to the lobby to put on my handsome tunic and shiny shoes and perform a perfectly rehearsed salaam for my confessors, those for whom it is my deep pleasure to offer solicitude.

Seven

Bum's Rush

My wife and I are fighters; we've spilled out of doorways everywhere in the city, stamping our feet and shouting—and given the likelihood that we've been witnessed by most of the population, apparently famous as such. We've spit at each other across the table at expensive restaurants. We've rolled down the aisles of department stores and airplanes and through the well-appointed rooms of other people's homes, pulling each other's hair and screeching. We've had public fights from phone booths, across the city from one another, each surrounded by a small crowd of concerned citizens drawn to the spectacle of us shouting and flailing, then collapsing to the floor of our booths sobbing.

We can't help it. We provoke and shove and snarl at each other, trying to draw up any kind of deep feeling. Love and bloodletting are equal enthusiasms, obligatory rites of attraction and repulsion. Any upheaval will do; we seem to think that we'll evaporate if we aren't at full throttle. We threaten each other, cry pitifully like children, shout, laugh until we're barking. We bill and coo. We have sex like cats. We sin grievously in bed and shout hosannas.

A firestorm, that's our general state of being. Communion is our only aim, by whatever means necessary. It's as if we keep hurling ourselves at one another, hoping that sooner or later our molecules will line up and we'll meld into a single being, achieving union at last.

"Why don't you two get help," a friend said angrily, having had enough of the poison filling the air. He's a smallish man. I was so upset during a fight that I tried to pick him up and throw him at my wife; failing that, we chased each other in circles around him, grabbing and screaming filth and finally laughing hard until he shouted at us to stop.

"Get help for what?" I said to the man later, looking bewildered. Of course I knew the answer, but it's our way as husband and wife, it's our troth. Other husbands and wives have their way; this is ours. Let anyone who thinks we're ridiculous see if they can find a love as deep and abiding as ours. There is no love like the love that survives a fistfight.

Now we've come to a crisis. She's a small woman, a gamine, and I'm a large man—and fit. But she's become a devotee of all the passive resistance martial arts disciplines, and with no apparent effort, when she's losing a fight of words, she's come to be able to throw me across the room. I'm helpless against it, and the world is suddenly out of balance.

Her dojo is on the ground floor of our building; she began classes there after reading Sun Tzu's *The Art of War* at night in bed. Next to her, while I tried to keep my eyes from darting anxiously to what she was reading, I studied my books about the classical logical fallacies.

During the day I can hear the alarming shrieks from the women's classes below as I sit and read above. I always see it as an architectural elevation in my mind: a floorful of furious, rampaging, shrieking women demanding redress from a history of the bad behavior of men, at long last, and me above, tiny in my reading chair.

One day in our apartment my wife showed me what she'd learned from her sensei, a large, paranoid white man who, whenever we three happen to meet in the lobby, always manages to insinuate his body between us.

As my wife threw me again and again, I thought of the sensei and the women stopping class to stare up at the ceiling without blinking, spellbound, listening to the sound of my body crashing to the floor above. Her display was dazzling; and even though I was being thrown to the floor hard, and it hurt,

I couldn't concentrate on anything but her spectacle—fine, achingly pretty, so good at everything she does. When I told her this, she took it as a patronizing attempt to disempower her, as though as a woman and a person she is so without affect that I think getting brutally thrown to the ground by her is just an opportunity to study her.

"Try fighting back if you think it's so cute," she said.

"Now just a minute," I said, steamed and squirming. I tried to explain that I didn't think it was cute, that the pleasure I was showing, a result of my love and high regard for her, seemed to be able to coexist in a parallel reality with the pain she was dishing out, not a contradiction at all if you consider the human brain and its remarkable ability to think about more than one thing at the same time. Think of the Catholic saints, I offered: While they were being gutted they must have also been aware of the scale of the event, of its meaning and majesty; they might have, while being boiled, anticipated the beauty of the iconography that would illustrate their willing surrender to faith. But I was gripped by the impulse to laugh, suddenly self-conscious because she was studying my face suspiciously for any subtext it might reveal. She thought I was mocking her, we argued ferociously, and then she spent the rest of that day throwing me to the ground whenever we happened to be close enough for her to rush me. In the middle of the day, already covered with bruises, I approached her aggressively with as much dignity as I could muster, bravely coming within arm's length of her. I pointed a rigid finger at her chest and said this: *If you ever touch me inappropriately again, ever, in any way, I will strike you, I promise, woman or not!* As I spoke, she stared at the end of my rigidly pointed finger without blinking, like a predatory animal, and then grabbed the finger and somehow knocked me down again immediately, before the last words of my speech—*woman or not!*—which I had rehearsed behind the locked door of the bathroom while hiding from her, could be barked out to express my indignation.

By late afternoon I was running from room to room away from her, begging her to stop, crying out *I get the point, you win, for Christ's sake, you win, please stop.*

She wins every fight now. During our fights, of which there are many, and spectacular, and public, and everywhere, she'll use her martial arts on me when she's had enough of my polemics. Her sword is mightier than my pen.

We seem to have lost all of our friends; one of them got punched by accident when during a fight in a cab my wife took a wild swing at me; I ducked and our friend took the hit and her nose exploded. She shouted at the cabbie to stop to let her out, and then shouted at me, blood running from her nose onto her shirtfront, *Why did you duck!?* I tried frantically to explain to her how the limbic and the autonomic nervous systems work, how they caused me to duck spontaneously, how I couldn't have helped ducking; therefore the only willful and actionable act was my wife's punch, so it would better serve the cause of justice to blame her and not me—but she grew even more angry, slammed the door in my face, and we never saw her again.

There is a structure to our conflicts, to which my wife readily confesses as part of her agenda, revealing the fundamental difference between us and the source of the trouble: During an argument, when I finally make enough good sense, when I construct an exquisitely balanced and nuanced argument to support my position, when détente is imminent, when peace and good fellowship begin to rise from the wellspring of our excellence—instead of conceding the point, instead of bowing to me, instead of dropping to the ground and pawing me in supplication, instead of being grateful for my clarity, for my call to good sense and happiness, as she would if there were a scrap of righteousness left in this heartbreaking shit world, she resorts to physical violence. She calls me names and then knocks me down.

I'm a large man, and she can knock me down in a way that makes me crash to the ground. She sweeps me into the air and I land hard. She makes a little graceful, economical move, and I'm in the air; time seems to slow when I approach the top of my arc, in zero gravity, a moment to reflect upon absolute disempowerment and commiserate with all my brothers and sisters throughout human history, in every clime, who've felt the boot of one like her on our throats. And then I crash to the ground on my ass suddenly, arms and legs flailing. I usually *oof* when I hit, which will make anyone who is watching laugh. Even *I* laugh, because it is actually very funny, and because my wife, *mine*, is so strong, so adept, my feelings of victimization dissolve in adoration even as I crash.

I've suggested to her that she can't just knock me down whenever she wants, and she responds by saying that apparently she can. It's an affront to our fundamental idea of jurisprudence, I say, my voice rising. And therefore what, she says softly, passively resisting. What if everyone acted this way, I ask. They don't, she says. I'm struck dumb. I don't know how to respond to the brutal truth of her position. Six thousand years of philosophy and yet moral teachings and political science haven't yielded an argument that I might make to her regarding her brutality. Who cares if I'm oppressed? If she's beating me to death, and I call the cops, they'll come over and beat me to death too. She wins, no matter how elegant or pitiful my argument, no matter that I begin by using the classical logical fallacies to make my points, simple rules of orderly thinking that intelligent men have devised to live with some sense of decorum, no matter that I end whining like a boy, writhing pitifully at the hem of this woman, begging her to listen to reason. I get tears in my eyes with frustration just thinking about it.

"*It's fascism!*" I screamed during an argument. We had been arguing outside the entrance of a department store; I saw her ratcheting up for a physical attack. I screamed, "*Don't! Use your words!*" She shrieked back, "*YOU use YOUR words! Use them to call 911 for yourself, you little shit!*" Deranged by her piercing shriek, we flew into a furious dogpile, which lasted only seconds but it drew a crowd. We flew apart, and I shouted that in essence she was a fascist, she wanted absolute centralized authority, repression of opposition, and there was even a kind of nationalism in the form of personal conceit.

"You're a goddamn enemy of the state!" I concluded, but by then I was insane with frustrated rage and hoarse from shouting, and my speech ended with a squeak. She looked like I'd slapped her; she started to cry, sobbing that she *wasn't* a fascist. I gloated; I had gotten to her, I had reasoned with a mad dog. *"Hah!"* I shouted, *"This should be a goddamn national holiday! Fuck You Day!"* But still crying, not missing a sob, she suddenly swept me. I went flying, and landed on my face in the grass with my ass in the air. I might have gone unconscious for a brief moment, a moment she would have used to study the scene with colossal satisfaction before she rushed to me to see if I was alright. The crowd might have thought they were witnessing an allegory: The Horse's Ass Regarded by Woman Triumphant.

The crowd hated me for making her cry, and shouted encouragement when she floored me; while I lay there in the grass she told them, still sobbing and sniffling and choking pitifully, that I looked like the colossal fallen statue of a deposed tyrant. I was the fascist, she implied, not she, and the crowd agreed.

The witnesses liked what they saw: a presumptuous stuffed shirt getting knocked silly in the middle of his unsolicited soliloquy, his ass in the air, his poise demolished, the elegant architecture of his polemic reduced to an *oof.* And, more elementary, they witness a simple morality play, the story of a large, aggressive man, who bears all the mortal and venial sins of all men for all time in all climes, defeated by a tiny woman who brings to mind their origin, their mothers, their nanas and nannies, their pretty wives and sisters and daughters, even the mother of their god.

Later when we talked about the incident I had to give her a nod for maintaining the con; she might have shared the wiliness of her game with the small crowd by laughing and showing that she had tricked me with a form of the sucker punch; instead she continued to cry and argue her point and won a moral victory with them as well.

She can't be stopped, not within the received moral parameters of a man's behavior. In the vacuum left by the unthinkability of punching her lights out, I have only persuasion. It's left to me to circumnavigate her, find the trail of bread crumbs to her humanity, her font of compassion; and isn't this the aspiration of every chance meeting, every conversation with everyone, every day, anyway?

At an important person's dinner party, we got into a discussion about diet. It escalated to a disagreement, then to insults, then to slaps, and then we flew at each other, wrestling into a mutual headlock. We were so braided into a death grip that neither of us could make a move. The other guests tried to ignore us out of embarrassment as, still seated at the table, we held each other locked in the embrace. Eyelashes touching, we hissed and whispered violence to each other. *Let me go or I'll poke your eyes out, you idiot,* she hissed. *I'll poke yours out, you cow,* I whispered. She spit at me from an eighth of an inch away and I spit back. I started licking her face and laughing. *Ugh, you're so disgusting. I hope you die soon, you creep,* she whispered. *Ladies first, hag,* I breathed.

Finally everyone had had enough. Half the party jumped up and started pulling on me, the other half pulled on her; the two teams heaved without success. At last a disgusted guest grabbed the pitcher of ice water and emptied it over us. We were forcibly separated like copulating dogs. She started crying and asked the host to throw me out, which he did, and many of the guests shouted threats and cursed me as I ran to the door. I yelled back to them that she was equally at fault, don't be fooled, there is a grave injustice here, but they grew even more menacing, and I ran for my life.

When she got home, hours later, she told me that after I ran out she slowly sank to the carpet in grief and they all knelt and laid hands on her like a Pietà; they cooed to her and comforted her when, with her eyes big and wet and her cherry lips swelled, she weepily told them I was probably dangerous. I could see it; even I, as the antichrist in her story, would have been moved. She told them I was impotent, and that I couldn't read. She told them she would have left me a long time ago, but she had nowhere to go, and besides, as curious as it sounds, she couldn't help it—she loved me. She said she told them that she understood the pathology implied in the fact of her loving someone like me, but that it's the main theme of her therapy. And her therapist, a behaviorist, is confident that there will come a time soon when she will have developed the ego strength to leave me. She said they told her my behavior was barbaric and unconscionable, that they all hated me now, and they all offered her their cell phone numbers to call right away, any time of the day or night, if I start acting up. She said then she stopped snuffling, got up off the carpet, went to the bathroom to wash her face and freshen up, and had a good time for the rest of the evening. She added that the dessert was her favorite. It was yours, too, she said, but you weren't there to get some, were you?

"Why did you tell them you're in therapy? You're not in therapy."

"Oh, they loved it. They're all in it themselves, so they were all very enthusiastic. They each enjoyed telling me just how neurotic they were, their shrinks' specialization, and their diagnoses. They're all on meds."

"You told them I was impotent?"

"Yes."

"You know I have to punish you for that later."

"Oh, please don't, mister."

"And you told them I couldn't read? Well done. That is just high caliber. Really, well done."

"I knew you'd like that. They ate it up."

A pause.

"You told them that you love me?"

"Yes."

"You told those strangers."

"Yes."

"That you love me."

"Yes."

"Do you?"

"Do I what?"

"Love me."

"So much, sweetheart," she said, collapsing against me and putting her small, perfectly formed honey arms around my neck.

Here is the conundrum: I love this woman, no matter what she does, no matter how much pain she dishes out, and she loves me, no matter what I do. We're not masochistic; it's more that our daily relations seem to exist in a parallel universe, which I watch from a distance; during a fight, as she rushes toward me to do violence, I regard her pretty, intelligent face and her lithe body for as long as I can before the blow.

"You're a fool," I said during an argument.

"No. Women can't be fools," she said.

"Oh, is that so? Why not? I can't wait to hear this. Tell me why you think a woman can't be a fool."

"Because only a man can be a fool. If you say a woman is a fool, it means usually that some jerk is hurting her and she won't leave him. It's generally agreed upon that a woman can't be the kind of fool you're talking about."

"By whom?"

"The general public."

"Oh, you took a poll?"

"No."

"Then how?"

"How what?"

"How do you know?"

"How do I know what?"

She's toying with me now, slipping away. This is a sign I'm making sense, and therefore she will consider some kind of physical action. I stared at her.

"How do you know," I said carefully, my arms slowly rising up to protect myself, "that it is a generally held belief that women can't be fools?"

"I just do."

"You just do?"

"Are you deaf?"

"You can't just say 'I just do.' I've got a whole polemic here and it's your responsibility as my wife to engage in it. Pay some attention, for chrissake. Are we trying to figure something out here, or not?"

"Oh, you mean if I'm a fool or not? Okay, that makes sense. I'm fair. Take your shot."

"Okay, well, if an individual believes someone, anyone, is a fool, or attributes any qualities at all to them, it's a judgment. And since all judgment is subjective and implies in and of itself that an objective reality can't be apprehended, it doesn't have to stand any test of objective truth. If I think a woman is a fool, it has to be added to the menu of possibilities for the description of that woman, because all it takes is one person in the world to think so. There actually is no definitive you. Regarding *you* in the world, there is just an ocean of shifting, autonomous perceptions. Even your self-knowledge is insubstantial. The world is composed of a loose aggregate of subjectivities, which I think is the great mess and the great tragedy of being human, but there it is. Objectivity is just an expedient way to get along. You're a figment in a churning universe of figments. And in my opinion, in this moment in time, also a fool. So. I make a syllogism: You're a fool, and you're a woman. Therefore women can be fools. Voilà. Amen. Admit it. And admit the beauty of my argument."

She stared at me with nothing in her face.

"What the hell are you talking about? You just said nothing. Hee-haw, that's what you just said. I'm a fool? You're a nothing."

"I'm a nothing? I am most certainly not a nothing."

"Yes, you are. Less than nothing. Regarding you, I feel only horror. No—indifference. I turn my back on you."

She turned around with her back to me and folded her arms across her chest.

"You're dead to me," she said.

I stared at the lovely slope of her back, her shiny hair. God, what a good-looking woman. I'm the luckiest man on earth. Tonight, when I'm not dead to her anymore, I'll see if she'll let me do it to her from behind.

Heavy-lidded with the thought, I didn't realize she was

suddenly rushing headlong toward me. But that curious sensation of time slowing down made me absolutely certain that, just before the crushing bone-to-bone impact of the head-butt, I could feel the soft skin of her forehead on mine and I thought she had come rushing, in an impetuous convulsion of love and kindliness, to caress me.

You don't have to be very strong to give someone the bum's rush in the classic manner. If you grab the victim suddenly by the pants and the collar, and yank up, their arms dangle foolishly, the pants are up the crack, and the physics of the thing are such that they are virtually immobilized; you can do what you want with them. She threatened to walk me into traffic once. I was trying to defend myself during a heated disagreement on the street in front of our apartment building by invoking an obscure logical fallacy, using its Latin name. She went quiet and looked at me with an evolved hatred and whispered, *I'll kill you this time, you ridiculous little gasbag.* Suddenly she was behind me. Gripping my pants and collar she rushed me toward the street, which was roaring with traffic. Anticipation of my death loomed and as we rushed forward my life passed before my eyes. And when she didn't actually cast me into the traffic my relief was so great I laughed out loud, breathlessly and explosively barking to her which episodes of my life I had seen; she caught the humor and we laughed together, hard, purple with joy, squealing in alto and bass counterpoint. Then we ran inside our apartment and had sex like a fistfight, careening around all the rooms as if we were killing each other, breaking things, crying and shouting. Then we slept the sleep we seek, on our stomachs with our faces buried in the pillow, pressed side by side, head to toe like two stuffed piglets at a sow's teat.

That night I had this dream:

I carried her baggage, an enormous sack consisting of everything she owned. Like a Volga boatman I pulled it behind me along the tarmac toward the plane, with a thick seaman's rope over my shoulder. She insisted, even though she was leaving me, that I do so. When I suggested to her that if she was leaving me it seemed more just that she should really carry her own baggage, she shouted me down.

"Don't you dare put that luggage down, you little halfwit!" she shrieked at me. "I hate you! I hate hate hate you! I . . . just . . . HATE you!" I could see her uvula waggling. She turned to the crowd. "I HATE him!" she shrieked.

She had chosen as her destination a tiny Chinese village which her research revealed would be exactly on the other side of the earth from our apartment, as far away from me as she could possibly be and still be on the planet.

She climbed the steps to enter the plane; at the top she turned and looked back at me and shrieked, "I hope you die soon!" and to the crowd, "Somebody kill that one!" She entered the plane and slammed the door as if it were her own bedroom.

The plane taxied and took off; as it circled back over the airport, she looked out the window and saw me standing on the tarmac, head down, shoulders sagging, inert, in the position she had left me. Her rage and contempt for me were so great that she suddenly punched out the window so she could give me a vigorous middle finger from shoulder to fingertip, the last image of her I would ever see.

She was immediately sucked out through the tiny window and dropped through the air toward me where she landed right in my arms.

"Hurray!" I shouted in the dream, and out loud into the room. "God loves me!"

"Me too!" my wife shouted into the room, from her own dream.

Eight

🪶

A GODDAMN INFINITE EMERGENCY

1

I'm a professional letter-writer; that is to say I write letters for a living, for men—specifically men in trouble, men to whom words don't come easily, illiterate or laconic men who don't trade in words. I think of them as my brothers, and my heart goes out to them.

Letter writing is an ancient and distinguished vocation. I'm very good at it, I'm always happy to tell everyone all about it, and there it is, I don't mind saying so. I think a little bit of conceit is reasonable for a gifted man. Modesty seems smug to me; when someone makes a showy display of it, a little smarmy grin, hands folded unctuously in the lap, I just want to kick them.

It's hard work. If a client wants to make an argument, I need to bring to bear all my knowledge of polemics and ethics and the classical logical fallacies. I need to know some rudimentary psychology, some sociology, philosophy. I need to know all about the reader; if they're described as difficult or narcissistic by a client, I need to be cunning, to slip and slide past their conceits and bleed into their consciousness with words. One time a man, demonstrating the very reason he had come to make use of my talents, in his rage could only describe the reader as "a cow," and I had to think about that.

If a man wants to seduce the reader, I'm his Cyrano, giving voice to his lust, and consummation is the only reasonable critique of my work. If the man successfully seduces the reader through the agency of my letter, then it was a good one, a terrific one, and I feel very attractive—as if I myself had wheedled the reader and had sex with them.

I'm very talented at invective; if a man wants to offend, if he wants to tell the reader to go fuck his mother, I will accommodate him. I'm his champion, his angel, and the problem of propriety is his. It's his voice, and in order to write a successful letter I need to strike an empathic relationship with him, whom I think of as a fellow traveler, my brother; and anything less than a consummate success is to abandon him to his agony and me to mine, a grief peculiar to all men, an unsympathetic race even to themselves.

2

I'm unable to write letters for women. I have been told, by women pink and puckered with rage, that I know nothing about their gender. I always try to be as attentive as I can be when I'm in conversation with a woman, but it's true that as yet I can't claim to have truly understood a single thing I've heard from or about them. During our conversations, when I'm using all of my powers of observation—leaning into them and looking right into their eyes, furrowing my brow and rubbing my chin and making the attendant sounds of interest, trying my very best to imagine the exotic world they're trying to conjure, and trying, Jesus help me, trying, as I've been told, not to think about how pretty they might be, or about their sequestered breasts or their secreted vaginas, or how their resplendent hair falls perfectly at their shoulders like a shiny bell—a woman will look at me quizzically, as if I'm insane.

Even as a small boy I was thought of as insane by my own mother and aunts. I know myself to be basically a kindly man, if a moody one, and certainly I was as kindly and charming a little boy as boys go, with a little sweet face and fathomless dark brown eyes and long black lashes and a flaw apparently attractive to them in the form of a tendency to cry all day long, every day. Oh, I remember: the lavish pleasure of the sob, the almost libidinous heaving of my tiny chest, the limpid tear and its gleaming punctum of light, one in mid-passage on each cheek, and the advent of self-love, arising from birth itself, the first eviction, the first lonesome gasp of breath—the first insult! There are photographs, and I'm crying in all of them; the lashes glisten and the eyebrows peak in the middle piteously like hands in prayer, unconsoled. I was beautiful in my grief. But I listened hard, given that even then I knew they were my angels, and were trying their very best, only for my safety and well-being, to explain to me how things worked, so I haven't been able to account for their conclusion that I was insane. And, as all men do as they age, I've come at last to think of most of their advice, although crudely put and shouted en masse into my crib, as right on the money.

I think only a man can find the right words and the right beat and certainly a sympathy for men and their agonies to be able to give voice to their sentiments. A woman, I believe, even in the name of charity, even in the name of compassion, might helplessly listen to a man only through the lens of her rage and then misunderstand everything; a reasonable rage, I'd have to say, given the generally poor behavior visited upon her by men, always and in every clime. Empathy and therefore communion are not to be had between the genders—a great misfortune.

A man is given to believe he is responsible for certain ways of being, which he learns from his father, and his peers, from history, from books, the newspaper, the TV, everywhere and always; he blunders through the day in a particular way. He has a *penis,* for Christ's sake, in a world that believes all iniquity is represented by it—the sorry, withered thing, hanging down and waggling pathetically and uselessly from side to side in the dark all day long, like a little wrinkled and lonesome worm looking hopelessly for its mother, as its dimwit of an owner wanders stupidly through the city, through the day, uncomprehending and making trouble for everyone, and then called into service later at night for obligatory responsibilities regarded, in each and every way, as dissolute and debased. The implications of this alone must cause a man to come to a distinctive way of thinking about the rooms and cities he crosses, about the very people whom he loves, the very people with whom he would like to commune, and by whom I'm hired to find the words that describe how he feels by way of a letter—giving rise to a mind-bending conundrum, because it really can't be done, words are never the thing. A kiss is the thing, a kick in the face is the thing, but a word can never be the thing.

No less a philosopher than the luminous L. Wittgenstein wrote that language itself is the single impediment to understanding the nature of things. And Socrates—Socrates! Before even the invention of pants!—said that once a word is chosen to describe something, one can never again see the thing it describes. When I read those words, which I do again and again, my heart sinks; to me this is the great and poignant tragedy of being. How can we ever hope to *explain?*

3

It's always my great pleasure to root around in words, which I think of as molecules of consciousness themselves. I can't be happier than when I sit alone in my reading chair, reading, ruminating, sounding a word when I come upon a good one—a juicy or a pungent one, rolling it around my palate like a piece of candy, wondering about how it came to be. Other men have sports, or Jesus, or who knows what; I have this.

The big chair is the special place where my elaborate rituals of pleasure happen; overstuffed, a beautiful reddish-ocher brocade decorated with a pattern of the heads of Irish setters. It's longish like a fainting couch, an allusion not lost on me as I sink deeply, as if I'm swooning, into the little sea of handsome dog heads. I always feel very small in it; if I burrow all the way in, my feet barely touch the floor. I feel like a boy in it. A happy boy. No one else sits there, and I think about that.

But now I'm having a crisis; something happened, and now I've become so doubtful about the efficacy of words, about their ability to mean what they hope to mean, what they *need* to mean, that I can barely speak to a man behind a counter, much less find just the right words, in proper syntax, inflected just so, to rescue a man in trouble by way of a letter.

I remember it exactly; I lay on the fainting couch–like chair, deeply into my little rituals, bundled like a papoose in my lemon-yellow Chinese silk robe produced from the direct genetic line of a rare silkworm larva smuggled out of China to the West in the nineteenth century. I wear it only on my chair. On the little antique end table inlaid with bird's-eye maple and teak sits a pot of 1999 vintage Minghai Beeng Cha Pu-erh tea served in my hand-painted porcelain Herend teapot in ultramarine-blue and white, with tiny attendant cups and muscovado sugar cubes from Barbados. And little home-baked Kirsch-flavored cakes of my own design and recipe—as aesthetic as they are toothsome; I'm very talented at squeezing a perfect blood-red flower blossom from my pastry bag in one pass. I'm very happy as I prepare for this pleasure; I suit up, bake the little cakes, brew the tea, and clean. I whistle as I work.

I have a habit of seeing myself from an elevated view: nested deeply in my chair with a full stomach, my books, my tea and cakes, my beautiful pictures on the wall, my wife—my pretty princess—in the next rooms, the fulminating city, the continent, the emerald-and-blue planet. In this kind of moment the world is good. I can't be happier than this. This is happiness.

That day, however, it was as though the machine in my head that sees to language started to smoke and shriek and fly apart.

I was thinking about a word; it had a beautiful sound to me, like a hum, or a murmur (beautiful, onomatopoetic words in themselves), vibrating my temples as I spoke it, again, for the libidinous pleasure of the thing—and again, and again, and again, and suddenly it collapsed, as if I had mined it too deeply. I felt like a heart surgeon pulling back layers of the heart thinking I'd find love or courage or strength—but finding only sluices and valves, a bloody mess. Immediately like a virus my doubt bloomed to include language itself.

Since that moment any word threatens to become a Babel-like nightmare, a quicksand of infinite possibility of meaning. I think I don't know what I'm saying and I think I don't understand anything being said to me.

I've been sulky at home, and difficult, given the bad mood that always eventuates from this kind of crisis, and my wife is upset. I start arguments, of which lately there are a multitude, given my goofy predicaments, none of which appear to make a scrap of sense to her. My mood spoils our beautiful home, she says, where there is affection and kindness and good food and good talk to be had, if only I didn't have my moods. She says my idea of an argument is infantile; I'm bombastic, I don't listen, I rant and whine and posture, I construct voodoo dialectics, I deliver Talmudic *pronunciamentos.*

"You act like a *child*," she responds, the enunciated word like a slap, humiliating me, refusing even to address the issue at hand, so contemptuous is she of my whole person in those bitter moments.

"I've had a *bellyful*," she cries, and I think about that: a belly full of what? What happens as a result of having had a bellyful? What is she trying to say to me?

Now she has insisted on new rules of engagement:

1. During an argument, there will be no running out of the room to my etymology books to do some fast research on a word that she's used. I understand the awkwardness of it, how it might impede the flow of a conversation; but how can I make myself understood if I don't understand what's being said to me?

Once, making fists, she cried, "You *oaf!*"

I ran for my etymologies, to home in on the essential meaning, the filet mignon of the word.

"So, I'm an *oaf,* am I," I said as I ran back into the room waving my book around, "from the Norwegian *alfr,* through the Old Norse *elf,* hence, a 'misbegotten, deformed idiot.' How can that be? Am I misbegotten? How so? Am I deformed? You can see that I'm not. An idiot? Please."

But, the new rules having been delivered with fists, through clenched teeth, with an underlying threat of abandonment, I'm now required to remain engaged and show evidence that I feel her sting.

2. There will be no invoking of the classical logical fallacies during arguments, which, if memory serves, although a fine polemical device, never seems to sit well with anyone with whom I've quibbled. And if I use their Latin names, it seems to make them even angrier. The language of logic and reason, invented by sensitive men to achieve communion, which should rule the day, seems to make them just furious.

"Hah!" I shouted once, "a tu quoque fallacy!" My wife

glared at me furiously, and then turned her back and put her fingers in her ears. This is a very painful gesture to me; with it she tells me that I am not in her world, and in a way it reminds me of the terrible knowledge that existentially it's entirely true that I'm not, I can never be. I can be made to feel heartbroken easily; I'm a wordsmith, a 'laborer of the word' as it's been knowingly called, one who lives in the profound and agonizing gap between souls, between whole, lonely universes, aching to commune, and suffering the inherent poverty of language to do so. As we all do, certainly; but for me, for whatever reasons of nature and nurturing, the gap is wider and deeper. I know my wife loves me—she is generous with her kisses and endearments—but her gesture aggravates my loneliness.

And, as a most ironic response to my elegant, nuanced, carefully researched and articulated reading of the situation—in *Latin,* for Jesus Christ's sake—she sticks her pointers in her ears, like a child or an idiot, exacerbating my crisis of language.

3. Under no circumstance will I shake a finger in her face, or in her general direction. I may shake my finger in the air or at God or at the ceiling, but never again in her face. I have tried to explain to her that it is a gesture of emphasis, not intended to demean, but she is not having it. She can't help it, she says, that a more primitive part of her brain seems to be engaged by the spectacle of a finger waggling in her face—an uncontrollable, atavistic, mammalian response that makes her

want to snarl and bash my fucking head in—which she may do sometime, she says, if I don't stop.

4. Although sometimes an expletive—a salient and rude word or phrase *meaning* to offend, delivered with a mammalian gesture of aggression, like the baring of teeth or a glare—may be the perfect and only way to articulate a thought, it is according to her a form of violence, and it has no place in civil discourse or a loving home. There is, she claims, no adequate riposte to an expletive other than an obligatory punch in the face, thus making the expletive essentially useless as a polemical device. If I shout *you motherfucker* and she punches me in the face, I have no recourse; the conversation is at an end. Here I invoke the holy moral fundament: A Man Does Not Strike A Woman. Even a tiny, helpless, and blameless man, a feeble or crippled or ancient man, a blind and mute man hoping to judiciously and righteously redress the most egregious of offenses, the most noble of causes, does not strike the largest, healthiest, guiltiest, most wretched woman, Amen.

5. No fancy vocabulary is allowed: I must be *pissed off*, I must not be *splenetic*; I must be *so angry I could shit myself*; I must not be *choleric*. No whispered asides to an imaginary colleague are allowed. No circumspection, no circumlocution, no laughing to myself without explanation. No making of fists, no stamping of feet, no sarcasm, vitriol, tirades, ridicule, sneering. No whining, whimpering, weeping, keening, shrieking, spitting, speechmaking, name-calling, or rolling of

eyes will be allowed.

I've tried to convince her that my way is an important way to be; I've begged her to consider joining me in reading the newspaper in the mornings; she would see immediately that a tantrum, a vigorous cri de coeur, is an entirely reasonable response to the terrible state of things any and every day on every land mass and body of water, so moribund is the world, so dissolute is the race. In the breakfast nook, our staging ground for world revolution, from which one thrilling day we'll rush into the street shouting at last, we'll rage on into the morning.

"This will not stand!" she'll shout.

"Tell it!" I'll cry.

"Right on!" she'll bark.

"Amen, sister!" I'll cry.

"Fuck the Man!" we'll cry together.

The new rules take from me both my defense and my offense, leaving me mute and impotent. A conversation about who might do a small domestic job is a wormhole of inexhaustible linguistic associations, and as I collapse into it, she leaves the room in a huff of disgust.

Then all that's left for me to do is *pule*—a tiny, prelinguistic sound—just loud enough to be heard from the other rooms, after which she returns to rescue me, understanding it as a cry of capitulation, arms open wide and love in her pretty face; she is, as I say, a good and kind woman who simply wants the best of things, and I'm grateful.

4

Now I move as slowly as I can on my way to my office in the mornings, my heavy head down, inching through the city, making a wrong turn, stopping to greet a dog or have a long look at a baby, hoping to fall down and crack my head open—anything so I won't have to go.

I fight my way through the city, through the day. I don't understand what anyone is saying to me, so I divine that they are not likely to understand what *I* have to say either; this makes the simplest social intercourse a precarious event. I shout at the counterman at the coffeehouse because I think he won't understand my order. *"Cappuccino! Cappuccino! Whole milk! Whole milk! Steamed, for Christ's sake!"* I shout; but I've learned that balled fists and a shriek are not the best way to inspire good service. I shout endearments at my beefy, belligerent old mother (maybe the genetic seed of my own bellicose nature) on the telephone. *"I love you, Mommy! Do you understand what I'm saying here, goddamnit?!"* She shouts back: *What "Who is that?! What?!"*

Early in the mornings at the coffeehouse I get into fights with my associates, because when we converse—although they're all very bright and superbly educated men, and they all speak grammatical English fluently, in syntactical sentences, using appropriate inflection and body language—I don't think they're trying very hard at all to say what they really mean, what they really feel, so I'm sure I don't understand what they have to say. They may as well bleat. This causes a very troubled feeling, a kind of anxious lonesomeness, as though I'm looking through a telescope at an empty world, as far away and silent and melancholy as a satellite. This makes me frightened, and then angry, and finally when I jump up out of my seat choking on my spleen and spitting coffee—shouting across the gulf, demanding that they make themselves clear, stamping my feet and smacking the table for emphasis, rattling the cups and spoons and frightening them and everyone else in the place; when I shriek that they've grievously failed their intellectual and social responsibilities, when I bellow that they need to concentrate and take a goddamn breath and try to make some goddamn sense if they want to have a conversation with the likes of *me,* like stupid children they scream back at me all at once that I'm a bully, that I need to stop slapping the table and use my words. And then one, always the same one, a diplomate in Boolean mathematics, for Christ's sake, a goddamn Nobel Prize finalist, to whom as a *scientist* the vagaries of language should be anathema, and so should know better, runs to ask the very old and tiny proprietor to throw me out. The old man does so every day with gusto, the little shit, exercising his power as the proprietor, knowing he is protected by his age and frailty, and the law.

"Let's take it outside, buddy," he wheezes, a cheap phrase from old movies I think he loves to hear himself say, as he pushes me toward the door with a tiny, cold, speckled claw of a hand on my back to steer me while I shout, *"Don't touch me! Don't touch me!"* As I'm given the bum's rush I have an elaborate fantasy of punching the man's lights out, which, of course, I can never do, given the moral dimension entwined in the power differential; but the fantasy is a satisfying work in progress. In it I give myself a handicap, like a stutter or a hump to even the playing field; *Oh, he has a hump,* witnesses will say, giving them pause in their rush to vilify me for beating a tiny old man.

Every day I'm thrown out of the coffeehouse to continue my unhappy pilgrimage through the city, until there are no more associates to discipline, no more puppies to greet or babies to compliment, and I'm standing gloomily, my head hanging, eyes closed, on the street at the entrance of my office building, trying to draw up the will to cross the threshold. While I stand there paralyzed, the gaunt little foreign man behind the counter at the laundry next door, who apparently has taken some kind of interest in me, watches me with what looks like sympathy; he does something with his eyebrows at me, something more intimate than I ever have time for, thank you. Also behind the counter are his large, frightening, mustachioed wife and their spawn, a horde of what seem like scores of small, unwashed tots, all of them with chapped pink foreheads, greasy tufts of hair, identical gobs of snot plugging ghastly pug noses, dull in the eyes and dirty around the mouth; they watch me too, following his eyes. I resent them; all I need is the advice of more desperados, in this case foreign ones, on whom the nuances of the language will certainly be lost.

Finally upstairs, in the office at last, I thrash and sweat at my desk like I'm digging a hole. When I write, I know that whatever word I choose, there's another that's more to the point, if only I had the genius to draw it up out of the ether, the endurance to keep mining my notes, my thesaurus and dictionaries, my etymologies, books of quotations, books on linguistics, ethics, psychology, and of course my intuition, my art, trying to find just the right word, the one that might make the pilgrimage whole, undiminished, across the colossal universes between a man and his estranged loves, the one that will shake the reader by the shoulders and make them swoon and submit. It's a job of alchemy, wheels within wheels, and most of every day I sit at my desk struck stupid, stifling in the hot little room, a goddamn infinite emergency.

Every word is an unnecessary stain on nothingness an unhappy Samuel Beckett said; I've had these words embroidered in needlepoint and framed. It hangs on the wall right across from my desk, and I look up from my toil and read it over and over during my gruesome workday, trying to look into its genius, trying to accept the futility of my work, of words, trying to find a reason, at long last, to just shut up, to run back down the stairs into the street to my home, directly to my bed, where I'll try to find new reason for having been given this minim of being.

There at my desk I exhaust myself, fall asleep in my chair, and have epic dreams of being chased down the street by a cabal of furious associates—the old proprietor, my wife, the laundry man and his frightening wife and filthy children, hosts of babies and puppies.

5

Every morning my assistant, Robert, arrives at the office an exact minute after I do, while I'm still gasping from the climb up five flights through the creaking, palsied old building. When I'm halfway up I can hear him enter the little lobby below and stop and gasp at each landing while I gasp above. We're both large men, and when he arrives we gasp together in our coats, bent over with our hands on our knees as if we're dying, he a minute longer than I, while I watch him. The predictable timing of Robert's arrival is so suspicious I think he might be hiding behind a pole on the street watching for me, and this thought alarms me.

I'm taken to fixations, and I confess that I've come to an evolved one regarding Robert; he is a spectacle, by anyone's reckoning, I believe—a large and very heavy man, a *fat* man, if I may use the uncivil word as a simple description, larval and pink, with trembling breasts and burly nipples and an ample belly button tenting his shirt, polished black hair parted surgically and his face scrubbed immaculate. His eyes are puffy slits and his mouth is a pretty little cupid's bow made of four tiny, shiny cherries. He looks like he might burst, like overripe fruit. He wears suits and his white shirts gleam; the effect is sartorial. He's especially fastidious; he forces me to look down and regard the pattern of perennial food stains on my tie and shirtfront, some quite old and apparently indelible, and I'm resentful that he sets a standard for grooming that I can't uphold, one that is regarded as virtuous. I'm thinking of wearing a bib at my meals, like an idiot, because of Robert.

He wears a wedding ring; it was only weeks after he arrived that it sent a gleam from the deep valley formed by two little mountains of pink, hairless digit. When I saw it, I realized that I had thought of him as neutered, a probable virgin; but this new information sexualized him. I tried to fight it off but I imagined a cartoon of pouting lavender bellies, an angry purple nubbin of a pee-pee peeking out just below them, and extrapolated that his buttocks were two ghostly white, hairless planets. A mean-spirited and childish thought but, having had it, now I can't stop thinking about that.

I've arranged our positions so that when he sits in front of my desk and transcribes, I can study him while he isn't looking at me, hoping to draw up through the murk something of the real man; but all I can imagine is a little solitary homunculus buried somewhere inside his bulk, whose nature never ripples the surface.

He has a kind of fragile beauty though, an otherworldliness, and the kind of gracefulness that large men sometimes have. In the afternoons, a little beam of amber light reaches him at his desk through the only window, and he looks like an angel. Sometimes he's an angel, and sometimes he's ridiculous; I can't make up my mind.

Robert's desk is in a tiny alcove to my right; I can't see him from my perspective when I sit at mine, save an elbow or the tip of his nose if I lean forward an inch. I can hear him breathing. We rarely speak, even though he's no more than three feet away from me.

He and I, the filing cabinet, the radiator, and the two desks fill the stifling little room, and if we're both up and about at once, we have to be nimble to keep from touching one another. I dread touching him. As we pass, my hands go up in front of my body and I crane my head away from him. Sometimes I imagine that I can feel his body heat in a kind of percussion wave as he passes. The bathroom is right next to my desk, and I try not to listen for his obscene privacies; I sing when he goes in, as I do when I hear him eating his foul vegetarian lunch at his desk. He eats curds out of a little plastic container every day; once while he ate them I thought I heard him low softly with pleasure, and I almost bolted out the door and down into the street, meaning never to return. He fills himself with curds every day, and now I can't stop thinking about that either.

I hired Robert because I have too much work, but I really didn't want an assistant; I need to concentrate, a fragile condition at best, already compromised by the regular sound of a man speaking next door. I can hear the measured, canned voice of business, but no content; I jump up as fast as I can to look through the keyhole to see what the man looks like when I hear the door open but by some uncanny confluence of chance and physics I've only seen a scrap of leg and an expensive wing-tip as the man turns left at the end of the hallway. I slipped out quickly once to see the gilded text on his door; American Systems, Inc., it said, frustratingly absent of evidence of what he might be doing in there; I thought of a silent suited man behind a proper desk, with proper features and manners, immaculate, a crisp part in his hair, his pencils and papers at the ready, performing an unnecessary function, the nature of which I would never understand.

The exposed plumbing pipe runs the height of the building, through all the floors and rooms, and when it roars regularly I can't keep the thought from my mind, is it a number one or a number two rushing past my head a foot from me? Or I'm filled with horror at the thought that the lovely secretary in the office two floors above, to whom I haven't yet had the courage to speak, might just have had a bowel movement. Even the sound of my own heartbeat can be heard between sighs, men's shouts and sirens in the streets, between Robert's lunch gurgles, between flushings, between interior ragings about having been thrown out of the coffee shop yet again or having another fight with my lovely, kind wife, or thrashing about the irreconcilable problem of language. So just knowing Robert is there—thinking, breathing, digesting—are impediments to my concentration. I've tried to put cotton balls in my ears, but when I do I worry that I might not hear an alarm or a bullet or a falling satellite rushing toward the center of my forehead or someone cursing me or some other sound warning of imminent catastrophe, and I pull them out frantically.

As soon as Robert arrived I realized my mistake. I didn't have the courage to fire him during his first minute on the job so I set about trying to pretend he wasn't there. For a time we communicated by telephone, from his alcove a foot away from me, during which he'd ask me questions about word roots or declensions.

"Who *IS* this?!" I'd demand when he called, insisting he give his full Christian name each time, hoping he'd conclude that I was insane or even dangerous, given that I was only inches away from him in his alcove as I shouted into the room.

"*Who?!*" I'd demand again after he articulated the syllables of his name carefully.

Finally I stopped answering his calls, hoping he'd stop trying to communicate with me altogether and just do his paperwork and be invisible until it was time to call upon him to transcribe a letter. But now he sends me interoffice memos asking me questions, or offering obscure words he'd found in his own research (he hasn't yet matured enough as a wordsmith to know that the obscure word is the very problem; of interest to a linguist or a bombast or a pretender, but it has no place in the effort to commune with a real man in trouble). He waits until I use the bathroom to drop them in my inbox. From inside the bathroom I look through the keyhole and see him tiptoe out of his alcove to do it, balancing his bulk on tiny feet shod in gleaming black oxfords; the old building groans as he makes his way. I don't answer the memos, but he won't stop sending them. I thought there was something odd about them; after a week I realized with a shock that they all had the five-seven-five syllabic construction of a haiku. *"Conundrum, sphinxlike/An Oxford don's Latin slang/unfathomable,"* he writes, and my discomfort about Robert deepens.

I compose letters out loud, standing up behind my desk. Robert balances his mass on a tiny folding chair on the other side of the desk and transcribes as I recite. Most letters have emotional content; I might gesture theatrically and become emotional to find the sentiment, to get into character, as it were, like a method actor. A word might not occur to me until I make the gesture that attends it, as if words can be found in the body as well as the mind, making fists or stamping my foot, say, or laughing hard, or shouting, or thinking about kissing or slapping the face of the respondent. If a man retains me to seduce a respondent with a letter, like Cyrano under the balcony speaking words of love to Roxanne through the puppet Christian, I will mine my own libido in order to find the words to arouse the reader. It's no wonder my work exhausts me.

Now my thoughts about Robert have evolved from fixation to a point of obsession. I think about him when I'm home and on my walks. I've had a dream about him.

When we work I can see in my peripheral vision that as he records my words he turns his head to watch me; incredibly, his mouth moves. I can tell he's thinking critically about my ideas and choice of words. *"Amanuensis sought,"* I had advertised, thinking that the antique word for a steno would be responded to only by an educated man who knew its meaning. At his interview, Robert announced with pomp that he had advanced degrees in linguistics and literary theory, which I thought would be very useful to me, a virtually uneducated man, but that was where I made my mistake; I soon realized that as a result of his fancy education he thought of himself as a thinking man, and he was having ideas of his own, as though he might think letter writing isn't a talent—even a divinely inspired one, perhaps—and this makes me very angry. Who does he think he is? They're the epistolary *arts*, for Christ's sake, a noble profession practiced since the thirteenth century, the venerated precursor of the novel, and I regard myself as an *artiste* of the form, something that can't be taught. Robert needs to learn that only one *artiste* at a time can occupy the holy place in which sentences are invented.

"Alright, *what!?*" I feel like shouting when his lips move, and maybe I will soon.

Late in the afternoon I stood behind my desk composing out loud, emoting and gesticulating frantically, as is my way.

"*Enervate,*" I cried out, "You *enervate* me! . . . No, no, no, a bad word," I mumbled, "sounds like its own antonym." I threw myself back into my books and notes; papers and sweat flew.

Robert made a sound; I looked down at him.

"Robert?" I asked. "Did you say something?"

He sat, frozen, with his eyes down like a Catholic in a confessional.

"Robert? Do you have something to say?"

"Yes," he whispered, after a pause.

"And? What is it?"

He mumbled, his eyes still down.

"What? Robert! *Speak!*"

"I said I think it's a good word," he said quietly.

"What word?" I asked.

He whispered something.

"What? Speak *up*, please."

"Enervate," he whispered.

I was stunned; I looked down at him as if a dog had spoken. He looked up at me, and when he saw my face, he panicked; his arms flew up as if he was surrendering.

"Oh. I'm sorry, I certainly don't mean to imply . . . ," he said, red-faced and squirming like an immense, distressed baby.

"What do you have to say about the word, Robert?" I said through a clenched jaw with a forced patience.

His little cupid's-bow lips twitched. He made small wheedling sounds.

"Robert! Christ! Just say it!"

"Only that I think it's a good word, that's all," he said. "The *right* word," he blurted out, and choked.

"You do."

"Yes." His head dropped, spreading his chins across his chest.

"Well, it isn't. I don't like it. It sounds like the opposite of what it means. The reader is confused. The reader is *already* confused, that's the state of things, that's why he *reads*, for Christ's sake, to find some solace, to *understand* the sentiments of another citizen, who moves through the same travail, the same heartbreaking shit world he does. If he doesn't understand, he doesn't know how to feel or what to *do*. Words ought to try to resolve confusion, not be the cause of more."

"That's right. Of course you're right. Listen, I'm sorry. I shouldn't have—"

"That's right, you shouldn't have, Robert." I took the opportunity to address the larger problem. "Please, Robert, just do what you're paid to do, which is to write down my words, without offering your own, without speaking, without moving your lips, even. Because I can see you do it in my peripheral vision, and it makes me lose my concentration. I can't have distractions. I need to *concentrate*." I slapped my hand on the desk for the exclamation point, as I do in the coffeehouse, and Robert convulsed.

"The problem is that when you move your lips, I can't help trying to make out what you're saying; how could I not? It means you're thinking something, and then I wonder what it is you might be thinking, maybe you're thinking about a word I've used, which is outrageously presumptuous given your limited responsibilities, so I'm already upset; and then I wonder whether you're thinking of a word that's better than *my* word, and then I think maybe it is *indeed* better than my word, certainly an accident but entirely possible given the infinity of possibilities, if only I knew what the word was, and that makes me think about my crisis of language, which has grown to one of great proportions, and that makes me just want to go home and shoot myself. Do you see, Robert? I have a gift, Robert. I don't know how it came to be so, but I am the custodian of that gift. Finally why one word is better than another can't be parsed, it simply *is*, and that's why I can legitimately be called an *artist* of words, in that I am reputed to be able to find just the *right* word, one after the other. I have grave responsibilities, Robert, and I'm already half insane from the weight of them. A man's happiness and success hang in the balance when I write a letter, and I must bring my gift to bear as best I can for his sake.

"That's the way I need to have things—not the most fruitful arrangement for you, I understand, Robert, given your advanced degrees and an obvious, evolved ambition. But I think you should consider that the happy man is the man who is the author of his circumstance, whether or not it is regarded as a position of esteem; I suggest that at this time in your life you might embrace your position as my assistant with *enthusiasm*, and then you'll be happy. With all due respect to your person and your education, it's a one-banana job, and I would hire a monkey to do it if it could type. Perhaps you'll find that your art is to assist, to artfully serve. I think that's a dignified position, don't you? We are all the thing we've become, and who else are we expected to be? Someone else? Am I making myself clear, Robert?"

It was a beautifully articulated speech; I had drawn myself

up imperiously, looming over him like a statue of a local hero in a town square. I turned to display my best angle, which I had determined some time ago by placing myself between a tiny pocket mirror and the wall mirror in the bathroom; I did it when the lovely secretary moved in two floors above, to try to imagine how I might appear to her when I find the courage to approach. I used my best diction and inflection and syntax, and my most mellifluous voice to make the point. I've always thought that a subordinate *wants* to be dominated; that the secret desire of the second-rate man is to be left to his mediocrity, at long last. All he wants is a little beating, a little humiliation, occasionally, to remind him that he always exhausts himself when he tries to be more than a functionary at the service of a first-rate man.

But when I finished my speech, which I ended on a soft and generous note, looking above and beyond him into a utopian world of reason and good fellowship, Robert, who had been staring at me through his little slits in a maddening way, suddenly stood up, shaking. His face was a mashed cherry, a big sanguine lump of gore, electrified by the office-green wall behind him. It was a frightening spectacle; I had been thinking of him as a defeated man, a kind of hapless neuter, but I realized in that moment that even though he didn't look much like a fighter, and even though I'm a large and fit man myself, I hadn't anticipated his capacity for rage. If he went berserk in this tiny space he could use his best weapon, his greater bulk, as a juggernaut to crush the air and finally the last bits of life out of me. If he stampedes, I'll suffer internal injuries; blood will leak from my ears and my rectum. My wife and my associates at the coffeehouse will be exultant; they'll tell the story over and over, an epic morality tale in which I finally receive the chastening I had coming, and thereby they are redeemed.

Now Robert, the hero of their story, was a florid colossus filling the room, poised to redress their grief.

"What do you mean you don't like the word?!" he said indignantly. "Who are you to not like a word?!"

"What?"

"A word is not yours to like! It's not important that you *like* it! There's a job to be done!"

"But it's not the *right* word!" I said in a trembling voice, my crisis of doubt rolling over me in a wave.

"Nonsense! It means what it means! It means perfectly what we want it to mean. You're so arrogant!"

"Wait a minute here! What *we* want it to mean? *We?!* Who's *we?!*"

Suddenly I was furious; who is this giant and audacious sissy who calls me names and presumes to know best, who presumes to be a collaborator? My fear evaporated; I rushed around my desk to him, making fists. The office is tiny and we're both large men, as I've said; we stood belly to belly like yoked draft animals.

"Listen, you! *I'm* the goddamn boss here. His goddamn Majesty! And you're the hireling. An inconsequential hireling.

A monkey! *My* monkey! Just shut up and do your *work!*" I bellowed, an inch from his face, glaring hard into the little punctum of light in his eyes and getting spit on his gleaming shirt front.

"I don't care who's boss!" he bellowed back. "It's the right word! It means what it means. You have to use it if it means what it means!"

"*What?* No. No! I most certainly do not have to! Absolutely not!"

"Use it!"

"No! I'll *never* use it! How good could a word be if it makes you think of its antonym? A word that sounds like its opposite is a stupid word! I'll never say the word again. I'll never even *think* it again, it's such a shit word!"

"You—have—to—*use it!*" he roared, so loud it deranged me.

"Shut up!" I stamped my foot, shaking the room.

"*You* shut up!"

"How dare you!" I postured.

"Don't you posture at me, you idiot!"

"Don't call me names!"

"Idiot!"

"Stop it! Stop it right now!"

"NO! *IDIOT! IDIOT!*" he shrieked.

Stunned silence. I didn't expect that the vulgate would appeal to this fastidious, presumed man of letters; now he'd opened the door to barbarity, and I rampaged right through it.

"PIG!" I screamed.

More spittle flew from the explosive force of the hard consonant P. The word rang in the little room. I was out of control; I understood that calling him a pig was a consummate reckoning of his person that he'd heard all his life—that had certainly come to tears and beatings in his youth. He stared at me, the embodiment of a lifetime of torment, and suddenly his hand, as big as a roast, came up and slapped my face— hard. I stood gaping at him, disbelieving.

"What do you think of *that?*" he shouted, triumphant. "Does that contradict itself?! Any confusion about the meaning of *that?!*"

Now, having descended to an ancient, prelinguistic part of the brain as a result of the blow, with a will of its own my ham-hock of a hand came up and slapped *his* face; a ripple of flesh crossed it like a slow-motion wave, circled his head to his shaved lavender nape, and came around the other side. Stunned and outraged, he glared at me, the little pins of light in the slits aflame. Suddenly we flew into a furious slap-fight. We flurried and grunted and wept. Robert held his breath and turned purple, and he now looked like a giant colicky baby in a suit. I had correctly assessed his poor fighting skills; his eyes were shut tight and he blindly slapped at the air hoping to land one. While his arms were up in the air preparing for slaps I saw an opening and reached out and grabbed the front of his shirt in both hands to shake him; he shrieked and stumbled back, and the shirt tore away in my fists, buttons popping and flying across the room. He stood still, stunned, his hairless, lavender-white bellies and breasts now exposed, the tie intact between, pointing to an outie belly button as big as a crabapple. The burly rose nipples danced on their trembling summits. A beautiful sight if one could bring oneself to think of it abstractly. He stood shaking, fat tears on his cheeks, looking down at himself in a posture of humility like a saint regarding his own disembowelment. His tears gleamed like jewels in the amber shaft of afternoon light. This was the angelic Robert, and I felt suddenly guilty.

"Oh Christ, Robert. I'm sorry," I said, and I reached over to fuss with his mussed part and arrange the torn remains of his shirt to cover the luminous spectacle while he stared down at his feet, allowing me to. I felt a curious warmth for him.

"I'm so sorry."

6

The fight had exhausted both of us. We'd been as close as lovers; we'd touched intimately and cried out and smelled each other. Words had failed absolutely, aggravating my crisis; now it seemed to me that a crack across the head was the most unequivocal and poignant form of communication.

We both responded to the shock and intense intimacy of the fight by being elaborately gracious and formal. I tried to give a perfunctory nod vaguely in his direction when he did his work well, and his head dropped almost imperceptibly in gratitude.

"After you," I'd say to him, bending in a shallow bow, when we faced a passage too small for us both to pass at once.

"Oh, no, you first," he'd say, bowing a degree deeper.

"No, you," I'd say.

"But . . . ," he'd say.

"I insist," I'd say.

"Well, okay, if you really insist . . . ," he'd say.

"I do," I'd say, and he'd struggle past, holding his breath to draw in his bellies, trying not to touch me, for which I'm grateful.

"Thank you," he'd say, at the end of his passage, nodding once.

"Thank *you*," I'd say, nodding once.

We've begun to eat lunch together at my desk at noon. This was achieved wordlessly, in some way that is indescribable, by a lot of ahems and grunts and little nods and pointings, like two overweight cavemen in a tiny cave trying to settle in for the night.

We hadn't spoken or made eye contact for days. Finally, at our fourth painfully silent lunch, it was time to speak.

"Would you like to try a curd?" he asked in a tiny voice. "They're very good for you."

"Yes, I suppose I would," I said, and he rooted around to find a good one, speared it with his little plastic fork, and reached over with it. It was quite good, a little surprise.

"I see there's a Mrs.," I said, pointing at his wedding ring.

He looked up at me, startled; we'd never spoken about our private lives. He smiled, three simple creases in a stunningly wide pink landscape. It was a beautiful smile.

"Yes. Would you like to see a picture?"

"Sure."

He dug it out of his wallet, polished the surface with his napkin, and held it out to me. I reached out to take it but he kept a proprietary grip on it; I lost the little tug of war, and had to lean all the way across the desk to see it. The picture was of a lithe, elegant, and flawlessly lovely woman, utterly impossible to conceive of as a partner to Robert. I was so stunned a barking laugh escaped me and Robert looked up, startled. "Oh, I'm sorry, pardon me, I was thinking about something funny that happened another time. It was before we met. Far away from here. Let's have another look," I said, while he stared at me suspiciously.

He must have a secret, I thought while I studied her, to be able to have a woman like this, his appearance notwithstanding. Perhaps she has a trust fund, or a sexual proclivity for heavy men, or an attraction to intelligence that renders looks meaningless. I looked down at the picture again, imagined them embracing, her honey arms failing to make it all the way around his bellies, and the impulse to laugh bloomed alarmingly; I thought for a panicky moment I might explode in the man's face, but I successfully clamped down on it by grinding my teeth and holding my breath . . .

She was so lovely, the kind of woman that makes a man

think of love and domesticity, of endearments; as I studied her picture I struggled against the fantasy of gently kissing her all around her face, little soundless brushes of the lips the French call *effleurer* (the French, inherently artful and exacting regarding their language, have encoded kissing, bless them). I knew Robert was staring into my face, lingering hopefully, while I examined the picture of his wife, trying not to laugh, trying not to swoon. The clock ticked and the radiator hissed. I imagined us taking a walk in a pretty place, oblivious to the world. I imagined looking up from my reading to see her skirt flowing around her pretty legs as she passed through the room.

"She's a . . . *handsome* woman," I said finally, being very certain that I couldn't say she was anything else without something inappropriate entering my voice; I couldn't use a word that was glottal or labial or had any onomatopoetic relationship to lust.

"That's the word for it," I said, letting go of my half of the picture and straightening up, slapping the desk softly. "She's a *handsome* woman."

Robert stared the picture and then at me and then back at the picture. The little cupid's-bow mouth turned down.

"Handsome?" he said indignantly. "What do you mean?"

"What do you mean, what do I mean?"

"Well, 'handsome' is an odd descriptor, don't you think?"

"What's odd about it? Handsome is good. A good thing to be."

"Yes, but *handsome*, used to describe a woman, specifically somebody *else's* woman, is generally understood to be in lieu of the word *beautiful*, a kind of euphemism you use when you feel compelled to be kind, but in truth you don't think beautiful at all. And then I'm expected to finesse the insult by pretending it's a compliment. I believe you're trying to tell me, in some circumspect way, that you think my wife is *homely*."

"Robert! What on earth are you talking about? Handsome is good, under any circumstances. It isn't used except to define a virtue. There is universal agreement about—" My voice caught; now an image of the beautiful, elegant woman giving him a bath and powdering his ghostly white buttocks crashed unbidden into my brain. An eruption was close to the surface; little snorts of laughter were escaping my best efforts. My stomach was in a knot; I began to convulse, and turned away with my hand covering my mouth as if I was coughing politely . . .

"You're *laughing* at me!" Robert leaped up out of his seat, and I out of mine, remembering the sting of his slap.

"*No!*" My eyes began to roll up and I felt faint from holding my breath. I tried to remember painful moments from my past, lost loves, a holocaust, the death of a puppy . . . but I was lost to it; my will and resistance at last gone, I was swept to three stupendous, happy shrieks, so piercing that Robert, as if he'd been struck, stumbled back into the diagonal beam of amber light. He stopped, bathed in it; shutting his eyes in submission and cupped his breasts in his hands for protection, as if remembering our terrible fight. This was the Angel Robert, and I ran to embrace him.

"*Words are all we have*," said S. Beckett later, finally, directly contradicting his earlier dictum regarding the impossibility of words to mean anything at all, and I'm going to have it done in needlepoint and hang it next to its partner, as a sentiment of hope.